The Amigos

Tanmay Dubey is an IT professional based in Gurugram for over 15 years. After his hugely successful first book, *Just Six Evenings*, by Rupa Publications, *The Amigos* is his second book. When not busy spinning a yarn, Tanmay can be found reviewing Bollywood films on his popular Facebook page 'Tanmay's Movie Adda'. He loves running marathons in different parts of the world and is also passionate about long-distance cycling. He can be reached at authortanmay@gmail.com or on Twitter @Tanmay_Dubey.

Rahul Tiwari is an Electronics Engineer and after working in IT companies like Wipro and IBM for 6 years, he quit his job to follow his dreams. *The Amigos* is a part of his dream. He currently lives in Jabalpur, Madhya Pradesh, and spends his time as a farmer and an entrepreneur. He is a gamer by choice and loves travelling. He can be reached at tiwari.rahultiwari@gmail.com.

Praise for the Book

Tanmay and Rahul have written a witty, modern tale about courage and solidarity in the best and worst of times. Through their story, they capture moments everyone and every group of friends experience. This is togetherness in the best of times and the worst of times, wrapped in a captivating story.

– Sanjay Sinha, Executive Editor, AajTak and Channel Head, Tez

The book is very interesting. Tanmay and Rahul have done a wonderful job. I wish them all the best and hope they continue writing like this.

– Nawazuddin Siddiqui

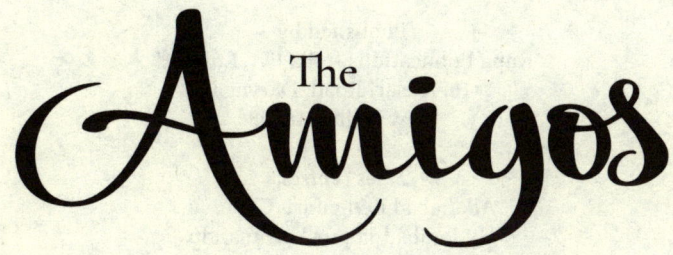

Tanmay Dubey & Rahul Tiwari

Published by
Rupa Publications India Pvt. Ltd 2017
7/16, Ansari Road, Daryaganj
New Delhi 110002

Sales centres:
Allahabad Bengaluru Chennai
Hyderabad Jaipur Kathmandu
Kolkata Mumbai

Copyright © Tanmay Dubey and Rahul Tiwari 2017

This is a work of fiction. Names, characters, places and incidents are either the product of the author's imagination or are used fictitiously, and any resemblance to any actual persons, living or dead, events or locales is entirely coincidental.

All rights reserved.
No part of this publication may be reproduced, transmitted, or stored in a retrieval system, in any form or by any means, electronic, mechanical, photocopying, recording or otherwise, without the prior permission of the publisher.

ISBN: 978-81-291-4533-8

First impression 2017
10 9 8 7 6 5 4 3 2 1

The moral right of the author has been asserted.

Typeset by Saanvi Graphics, Noida

Printed at Thomson Press India Ltd., Faridabad

This book is sold subject to the condition that it shall not, by way of trade or otherwise, be lent, resold, hired out, or otherwise circulated, without the publisher's prior consent, in any form of binding or cover other than that in which it is published.

PROLOGUE

Terror Attack at Tis Hazari Court, Delhi:
11 Dead, Over 50 Injured

Updated: 7 September 2011, 5.44 p.m.
(Source: NDTV)

A bomb, reportedly placed in a briefcase, exploded at the Tis Hazari Court Complex in New Delhi this morning, killing 11 people and injuring over 50. The explosion took place in the reception area at Gate No. 5, where hundreds of people had gathered to collect their entry passes. The Delhi Police will soon release sketches of the two suspects based on descriptions provided by eyewitnesses.

Home Minister P. Chidambaram has released a statement that The National Investigating Agency (NIA) will supervise the inquiry with a special 20-member team. An email received by different media organizations including NDTV said that the Hazrat-ul-Jihadi (HuJI) takes responsibility for today's blast. HuJI is a Pakistan-based terrorist group. 'We take the attack very seriously,' said NIA Chief D.C. Sinha. The email stated, *'We are responsible for today's blasts at New Delhi. Our demand is that our leader Arshad Guru's death sentence be revoked immediately or there would be more hell to pay. Watch out for your high courts and the Supreme Court of India if our demand is not met.'*

New Delhi

Monday, 10 October 2011, 10.45 a.m.

'The pigeons have flocked,' whispered the voice on the phone.

'Where is the nest?' the baritone on the other end questioned.

'Karol Bagh, Hotel Yamuna Palace.'

'Copy that.'

The man with the baritone voice hit speed dial on his cell. After three rings the line on the other side connected, 'Yes?'

'Sir, the suspects of the High Court blasts are in Karol Bagh, Delhi, holed up at a hotel.'

'Are you sure of the tipoff?' checked D.C. Sinha, Chief or Director General of NIA.

'I am hundred per cent certain. It has been confirmed. Need your orders for the operation.'

'Go ahead. I will complete the formalities, take your best team, but be careful, it's a public place. Minimum casualties, Major.'

'Don't worry, Chief, I'll be joining you for evening tea.' the line was cut.

Hotel Yamuna Palace, Karol Bagh

Monday, 10 October 2011, 12.20 p.m.

The four-storey building stood desolate at one corner of the buzzing channa market. The old hotel, adding to its seedy allure, seemed to be running low on maintenance, the outer wall paint chipped and was dirty with cracks in the walls. The usually busy street of the market was relatively less crowded today, Monday being the weekly holiday. The lane was lined with shops and hotels on either side, most of them shut.

A large black rodent scuttled its way in search of the food. It was careful not to be spotted by any predator. Smelling danger, it stopped with a jerk. The small legs of the mouse helped him scurry its way back to the hole in the wall of the road-side tea stall five-hundred-metres away from the hotel.

An autorickshaw stopped in front of the tea stall. Major Ritesh Dhawan from National Intelligence Agency (NIA) stepped out. He was dressed like a civilian—in denims and a crisp white shirt with the sleeves rolled up to the elbows, and sporting his signature Ray Ban aviators. He looked up and down the street casually as he paid the driver and picked up a duffel bag. His strong forearm muscles danced when he picked his bag stuffed with some clothes that were used as cushion for the guns stored inside. He slung the bag over his broad shoulders and walked towards the two men sitting around a small round table inside the tea stall.

Major Ritesh Dhawan, a Punjabi Jatt from Amritsar had joined the army five years ago and was one of the fastest recruits to get promoted from Lieutenant to Major, courtesy his heroic efforts in numerous counter insurgency operations in the Kashmir Valley.

With looks like his, chocolate boy but slightly rugged, and his persona including his academic excellence, he could have become anyone—a model or top-notch executive in an MNC. At 6.2 feet, strong, lean and athletic with broad shoulders, he had the ease of someone very comfortable in their skin. His eyes spoke volumes—dark, lidded and sharp, they didn't even miss the slightest action. Ritesh commanded respect by just being himself. His duty and dedication to the country was evident in how he held himself and his post, in how he treated his seniors and the men he commanded. Despite his young age he was an authoritative leader, a brave dedicated soldier and a courageous and compassionate human being. 'Being courageous is to have the heart to follow your own beliefs and convictions,' was his mantra in life.

As he reached the tea stall, he received small nods from his team, all in their '20s—Lieutenant Vikram Sharma, sitting hunched while glancing at the newspaper, Lieutenant Rashid Khan eating a matthi and sipping his cup of tea. His team had the benefit of appearing as casual civilians, with their non-military hairstyles and outfits. This team was the best Ritesh could have gathered. The three of them had been brothers in war for various covert operations across the country. All of them could almost read each other's minds and actions during a combat. A life-saving habit for them.

The tea stall owner, a Bihari migrant, was one of Major Ritesh's informer among many others in Delhi. These men were paid well by him for any important information they shared. Two days ago, he received a tip-off from him about the suspicious-looking men residing in Hotel Yamuna Palace for the past two weeks. In no time Ritesh gathered his men and took approval from the Director General of NIA about this operation. The DG has spoken to his counterpart in Delhi Police over hotline and informed him about the operation that his team was undertaking.

Lieutenants Vikram and Rashid had checked into the hotel on Sunday. What was originally a speculation, had turned into a confirmation this morning. They wouldn't have been able to discuss the strategy or chart out the plan of action in the hotel, for it was as yet unconfirmed if the manager of the hotel was an ally or a foe. It was also highly possible that the terrorists might be on a lookout for suspicious activity on their payroll.

As they sat in the tea stall sipping the hot brimming beverage, they saw the manager, Mr Bunty Walia, a short and overweight young sardar dressed in a bright printed shirt and matching pants stepping out and talking loudly on his cell.

'Sardarji might be compromised,' speculated Rashid quietly. '"Lazy and nikkamma", we overheard his dad calling him last night.'

'They've been underground for a month, possibly here. Getting mighty restless. They keep moving in and out,' added Vikram.

'You go on ahead, I'll check in after you've gone up,' Ritesh said in an undertone, looking at his watch, 'Reconvene in 10.'

Vikram and Rashid, quickly but without attracting any attention went into the hotel and to their room while the manager's back was turned. Ritesh, carrying his duffel bag, walked up slowly, pretending to talk on the phone, loud enough for a third person to hear. In his Punjabi Jatt accent, and essaying the role of a trade merchant he said, 'Oh, papaji, I've reached. I have got the samples of the clothes with me. *Ek din da kaam hai ji.* I'll be back tomorrow.'

Hearing his loud voice, Bunty Walia turned and asked Ritesh if he needed a room for the day. Ritesh walked in after the manager and signed up for a room. 'Manager saab, Room 103 please. Lucky number, you see.'

The manager accompanied Ritesh to his first floor room, offering to send the waiter with food and refreshments. Ritesh followed him in and quietly shut the door.

'Bunty, sit down. And listen to me very carefully.'

'Oye. What is this? Who are you? What do you want? How do you know my name?'

Ritesh removed his special issue 4th Gen G-lock 17 Pistol from the back of his jeans' waistband and laid it on the dressing table, 'Sit, Bunty. I won't ask you again.'

The door opened and Vikram walked in, carrying two duffel bags, 'Bunty,' Ritesh flashed a badge from his backpack and showed it to him, 'we're from the NIA. The National Investigating Agency. Anything you hear or see here is going to be classified. Do you understand?'

Bunty's jaws dropped open in surprise. He seemed a little shocked and a lot scared as to why these men were in his hotel. He nodded silently, his mouth open and eyes wide, as he saw Vikram unload the duffel bags onto the bed. Dozens of cartridges, guns and some technological gear spread out on his slightly dirty sheets.

'Do you know the guys staying in Room 203?' Ritesh asked, as he dragged a chair next to the bed and sat in front of Bunty, who started shaking his head even before the question was out. 'Do you recognize them? Who are they?' he pressed. Bunty swallowed hard, and looked from Ritesh to his teammate and said in a rush, 'I don't know them. They paid cash for a month and said they have some planting business so they need the room for one month. They keep to themselves. Room is never empty, no cleaning, no food. They bring from outside. We give only plates. But they paid a lot, so no one asked them anything. Sir, I don't know anything. Sir, let me go...'

He was interrupted as Rashid quietly entered the room carrying the check-in register from the front desk. 'They have checked in under aliases, paid for a month, names are not on record.'

Ritesh looked at Bunty Walia and told him to calm down. He picked up his G-lock gun and fixed the silencer Vikram handed him on it. 'Bunty, I know what papaji says to you. You have a chance to prove to him that you are a brave, courageous and a smart Indian. These men are the ones who carried out the bomb blast at the High Court last month. Will you help us in taking them down? The country needs a brave, himmatwala man like you. Do you understand?' Bunty, stared at Ritesh as his papaji's words echoed in his ears—nalayak, nikkamma, vella, fuddu...an ongoing litany. With a meek voice, he said, 'T...te...terrorists? *Main nahi,* sir. *Main nahi.* How will I? Let me go...'

For the first time since they sat down, Ritesh's voice took on an angry tone, 'Bunty, you are an Indian first. Punjabi later. For the first time, your country is expecting something from you. Be a proud Indian. A national hero. Be that man. We can carry out our mission, with or without you, but with you it will be easier and you will receive recognition as a national hero. Do you have G Mein D? *Gaand Mein Dum*? Decide now.'

This pep talk was enough to fill Bunty with courage and determination. His eyes stared back at Ritesh's with a new resolve. 'Go on paaji, I am with you guys. I will help you in all possible ways.'

'Fine, I need all your staff, waiters inside, no guests allowed till we finish the operation. Clean the entire hotel and wait for my orders. Is that clear?' Ritesh's authoratative voice underlined the importance of the situation. Bunty nodded his head and marched out of the room like an obedient soldier.

'Is he trustworthy?' Vikram questioned after Bunty exited the room, promising his cooperation.

'We need him for our operation to go smoothly, a bit about his father's reputation and being labelled a terrorist at the end really seemed to give him the much-needed resolve. Everybody has GMD—D can either be a danda or it can be dum. I just made him realize that it was time to take out the danda and replace it with dum.' answered Ritesh. 'He won't trouble us.'

'Status check. Get your earpieces on. Sync your watches. Is the tab ready and synced with the Sniffer?'

Ahead of it's time for Indian special operations, the 'Sniffer' was an indigenous design, by an IIT student adopted by Indian Armed forces. Like a dandia stick, except it could be extended outwards by a maximum of 12 feet, with joints every three feet, the steel rods getting thinner with every extension, much like a matryoshka doll. Connected via bluetooth to a specially designed palm tab, it could relay not only voice but also visuals from the tiny camera attached to the top end.

The three boys—Ritesh, Vikram and Rashid hid the Ka-Bar knife with its leather case tied in the shin and covered it with socks. The other arm, a 4th generation G-lock Pistol tucked at the back, hiding under the shirt.

'Here is the latest,' Ritesh said, laying out four 6x8 inch photographs of the suspected terrorists holed up in Room No. 203, 'Four guys, Wasim Mohammad Akram, a student of Unani medicine from Bangladesh; his brother, Junaid Mohammad Akram; a known Hazrat operative from Kishtwar; possibly a man of Iran-Afghan origin. This guy, the brother is a HAV.

The Amigos

High-value Target. The brothers are a priority. These two are the ones that walked boldly into our territory and placed the bomb. Need them alive. At any cost. They will definitely have knowledge about further plans and the HuJi's orders. The two younger, unknown operatives are supposedly Pathans from Afghanistan, nothing about them on file yet. Expendable. If caught alive, the more the merrier.'

'These two Afghani men are well built.' Vikram pointed at the muscular frames on the images.

'The stronger, the more enjoyable.' Rashid looked at them with a sneering smile.

'We've dealt with worse. Forty-five minutes tops boys. In and Out. Minimum casualties.' said Ritesh firmly.

Ritesh motioned for Vikram to engage the Sniffer. Vikram walked to the window and eased it open. As per their recce, Room 203 would be right above theirs, windows to match. He lifted the Sniffer out and started extending it, about three feet at a time. They would need a height of roughly 10 feet to be able to see inside Room 203. The windows were dirty but thankfully not tinted. In an instant, the visuals from inside the room were visible on the palm tab in Ritesh's hands. Ritesh signalled to Vikram to hold the Sniffer steady, the voice from within the room now reached them loud and clear, the four men in the midst of a discussion.

'Akhtar, you go and tell them that we are leaving Delhi by Thursday. It's been more than four weeks of playing hide and seek with these kafirs. One last plan and we will cross the border via Nepal. Everything is arranged for our exit. We will inform them of the next plan once we reach Nepal,' ordered Juniad. A tall, muscular Pathan, nodded as he got up and headed towards the door.

'Rashid and Vikram, follow this Pathan. Get him.' Realizing the size of the man, Ritesh ordered both his boys to take him on. Vikram nodded and handed over the Sniffer to Ritesh and sprinted out the door along with Rashid. Watching them go out of the room, Ritesh raised the Sniffer a bit, he wanted to see further into the room—one out, three to go.

'There is no drinking water in the room, call reception and get some water. Iftikhar, go and get some good biryani. This hotel serves shit food,' Junaid was marshalling his men.

Wasim, the younger brother, faced the wall while placing his order for the water. As he set the receiver back he noticed a strange shadow trembling against the light, reflecting on the wall in front of him.

He frowned, 'Hold on a minute.' Everyone inside froze at his tone, looked at him as he walked slowly towards the window. Ritesh realizing what was happening, quickly started to pull the Sniffer back. He saw Wasim's image in the palm tab getting bigger by the second, his hands reaching out to open the window. It was a race to see who commanded their hands quicker, Wasim or Ritesh.

Wasim's hand threw open the window and he poked his head outside.

A pigeon fluttered its wings and flew up off the AC box next to the window.

Stupid bird.

Ritesh was leaning against the wall, his heart panting, the Sniffer lying limp in his hands.

Good bird.

Breathing heavy at this close call, Ritesh too was suspended with tension. *I will have to take on this Pathan before he leaves the hotel else he may create problem for Rashid and Vikram.*

Ritesh ran towards the door with an intention to meet his quarry on the stairs of the hotel.

―∞―

Rashid and Vikram were following Akhtar in the barely busy street. The big guy, walking casually ahead of them, heedless of any surveillance, turned into a quiet by-lane, towards an old STD booth.

This was the perfect opportunity.

It was only the three of them in the lane. Rashid quickly walked past Akhtar, turned and said, '*Salaam walehkhum, miya.*' Akhtar looked up in surprise. '*Walehkhum assalaam,*' he replied in a thick Pashtun tone. Vikram, behind him, placed his G-lock's nozzle on Akhtar's back. 'Stay quiet. Things will be better for you.'

―∞―

Ritesh had taken no time to reach near the first floor stairs and waited for the big Pathan, who was descending the stairs slowly, swinging his arms and whistling an old Bollywood song. He stopped with a jerk as he saw a beam of red light moving up his torso and stopping at his forehead.

―∞―

Akhtar was quick, quicker than the boys had anticipated. He lunged forward planted a sharp jab in Rashid's abdomen, while using his momentum to kick back at Vikram. The pain causing Rashid to double up and Vikram to fall over backwards. With this split-second advantage and both his assailants down, Akhtar ran.

―∞―

'Don't even try, Iftikhar, you don't want to do anything stupid. Keep your hands where I can see them. Your head is my aim.' A deadly calm voice emanating from the darkness, surprised him. *Yah Allah! He knows our names, we are caught!* A cold sweat trickled down from Iftikar's temple. He was a greenhorn when it came to such situations, and this one had taken him by surprise. He was breathing heavily, his mind frozen, trying to figure out how this happened. Out of any alternatives, he decided to open fire and shout. *At least I can make my brothers aware of this attack.* Trying to use the cover of darkness, he slipped his hand into his pocket, reached for his gun and took a deep breath, preparing to shout, when one shot from a 9mm silencer fitted semi-automatic pistol hit his forehead. Iftikhar lifeless body thumped on the stairs, his expression unchanged.

Ritesh's large frame emerged from the darkness, his gun smoking slightly. He looked at the dead man, 'You had GMD, but not in the right measure, you should have learnt to use dum decisively, my friend. What a waste.' Ritesh threw the body over his shoulder and walked up to his room on the first floor. He dumped the body and after emptying Iftikhar's pockets, ran towards the reception to get an attendant's dress from Bunty.

Akhtar had not yet crossed the lane when he felt a searing pain in his calf. The shock, sensation and pain caused him to fall. He turned to see Rashid holding a raised gun with smoke coming out of the barrel while Vikram was almost on top of him. Vikram grabbed his collar and was about to knock him out when Akhtar landed a punch right to his stomach, throwing him off and to the side. Akhtar dragged himself up while holding on to Vikram and pushed him in front of his body, as a shield, his thick arm around Vikram's neck. *These two jokers would have been dead by now if only I had my gun with me.* He shouted at Rashid, 'If you come near to me, I swear in the name of Allah, this kafir will lose his head.' His other hand grabbed Vikram's hair in a chokehold as he started limping towards Vikram's gun lying five feet away. Rashid saw what Akhtar intended and started weighing his options.

Ritesh dressed like the attendant of the hotel knocked on the door of Room 203, his hand behind his back, feeling for the gun hidden under the waistcoat and holding a tray with a water jug and glasses in the other hand. He stood in a lazy posture looking most disgruntled. *They're probably checking who it is from the peephole.*

The door opened, 'Hello, sir, you asked for water?'

'Drop the gun, or else I kill your friend,' shouted Akhtar. Rashid looked at Vikram, his partner clutching at the arm that was cutting off his breathing. *Give me a cue.* Vikram's hand fell limply to his side. His fingers signing a drop and roll motion. Rashid nodded. Vikram understood, as he saw Rashid bent down to place the gun on the ground. *Now.*

Vikram jumped up and landed a kick on Akhtar's injured left leg. Akhtar groaned in pain and loosened his grip. Vikram dived to his left and the silenced shots from Rashid's gun hit Akhtar's chest and head. The Pathan stood still for a second and then fell like a log of wood.

Ritesh was about to place the water jug on the table when a low voice in his earpiece kept in the front pocket crackled, *Akhtar down, we are coming up.* His slight smirk did not go unnoticed by Junaid. 'What?'

'Oh nothing, sir. Do you want this near the window where you are or near the bed where your friend is?'

'There itself,' irritation spilled from Junaid's voice as he looked sharply at Ritesh placing the jug.

'You look new.'

'Yes, sir, I joined today.'

'You look and sound too smart to be a waiter.' Wasim got up from the bed, his hand reaching up towards Ritesh's shoulder. Ritesh was left with no option. He blocked Wasim's hand and punched him hard in the face. Wasim went down on his knees and cried out. Ritesh took out his gun pointing it straight at Junaid. 'Enough of this game, Junaid. You're done hiding. Iftikhar and Akhtar are killed. Your turn to surrender.'

Junaid bent down, pretending to surrender, picked up a chair and threw it towards Ritesh. Ritesh swept the chair to the side where it hit the mirror and broke, strewing the floor with pieces of wood and glass. He saw Junaid charging towards him. Ritesh bent low and tripped him up. Junaid crashed on the bed breaking it into pieces. Wasim meanwhile got up on his knees and reached towards a bag kept on the other bed. Ritesh kicked him hard on his face, breaking his nose. Blood spattered all over his face, falling flat on the floor. Unconscious. Ritesh turned towards Junaid... *Aaaargh*! Ritesh screamed. Junaid, who was hanging limply from Ritesh's arms, had shoved a small knife deep into his shoulder from the back.

As Ritesh dropped him, Junaid, breathing heavily, grinned and spat blood from his mouth. Ritesh clenched his teeth in anger and pain, his hand holding the bloody knife he had taken out of his shoulder. Throwing the knife aside, he jumped on Junaid, throwing him back against the wall and pounding his abdomen, face and sides. He felt Junaid's nose break under his knuckles, his ribs cracking as the punches came hard and fast, the wall behind Junaid cracked and got smeared with blood from the back of his head. Failing to stand up, Junaid slipped down on the floor resting his upper body on the wall. His face smeared in blood, struggling to breathe.

'*Aaaaaahhh...*' the sight of the mess, bodies on the floor, broken glass shocked Bunty Walia. He had run up to check what the commotion was. His fear rooted him to the spot.

'Bunty, I need you to get this cleaned up, we will take these people with us.' Ritesh couldn't complete his sentence as he saw Bunty's eyes looking at Junaid. He turned his face towards the terrorist, who was struggling to stay up straight. Junaid laughed, spewing more blood from his mouth, 'You will not get out alive.' Junaid lifted his hands. *What is that?*

Both of them watched as Junaid took out the belt that he was wearing and pressed a small button on it fitted with small plastic lumps, and held it up in his hand. As a cheap electronic watch beeped, Ritesh surmised it was either an explosive 1.2 or 1.3 which didn't have a mass explosion hazard but did have a projection hazard. He calculated his chances, Bunty was at the door, he couldn't let Junaid get the explosive anywhere near them. *The commode?*

It was the only option to contain the projection. He smashed his left elbow into Junaid's face, while grabbing the belt from his right hand, he ran towards the bathroom six feet away, the ticking of the bomb as fast as his racing heartbeat. Ritesh had barely taken three steps, when the ticking stopped. *I'm out of time.*

He threw the belt towards the open bathroom door as the bomb exploded with a deafening sound. The energy generated by the blast created a hole in the wall facing the road. Ritesh, too close to the bomb, got knocked off his feet and thrown against the window. He went down with the debris breaking the wall from second floor. The few people walking on the narrow street were taken by surprise, a knee-jerk reaction making them duck and run for cover. There was no major civilian causality. Bunty, Wasim and Junaid were knocked down but okay. Bunty got up gingerly, his ears ringing and face covered with dust, and moved towards the hole. He looked down at the street, holding on to the broken edge of the wall. Major Ritesh Dhawan, blood stained and unconscious, was spread eagle on top of the rubble in the street.

The siren ripped through the afternoon cacophony along the Ring Road. The ambulance was rushing toward AIIMS. The beeping of the machine, the only cue to life in Ritesh's broken body. A mask pumped oxygen into his lungs, supplying the necessary amount of the life support. The medical aids had administered morphine to ease the pain of his injuries. Each second of the clock was a race against time, marking each beat of his heart.

Ritesh gained consciousness once, about 10 minutes from the hospital, muttering incoherently, his eyes looking for reassurance. Vikram, seeing his distress, moved closer. He understood that what was troubling his leader was more than his injured body. He held Ritesh's hand and said clearly, 'They're in custody. Everything's okay. Mission successful, boss,' he ended with a cheeky grin. Relief shown clear in Ritesh's eyes. His body relaxing, he squeezed Vikram's finger, and closed his eyes.

CHAPTER 1

Aundh, Pune

Monday, 10 October 2011, 7.45 a.m.

The beeping of the clock was countered by a grumpy attempt to snooze the alarm. After a few minutes once again the attempt to snooze was repeated.

Forty minutes later the iPhone rang. A strong, muscular arm snaked out from underneath the white satin sheets to search for the device beneath the mess of pillows and blankets.

'Hmmmm...' Rahul mumbled.

'Rahul! Are you ready for your interview? Where are you?' a sharp voice checked.

'Oh shit,' Rahul sprang up, revealing his perfectly chiselled, unclothed torso and low hanging silk pajamas. 'I'll be there in five minutes,' he said as he threw the phone on the sofa adjacent to the bed and hurried toward the bathroom.

Seven minutes later he ran out the front door of his three bedroom rented flat with toast in his mouth, his long locks of hair, wet and gelled back and a business suit on, waiting to be buttoned. 'Rakesh, get the car ready,' he shouted. Rakesh, his loyal, old man-Friday stayed with him.

Rahul Bhatia was the scion of an industrialist, Rajesh Bhatia, better known as the 'Steel King' in the industry circles, the owner of Bhatia Steel Pvt Ltd. Rajesh's father, Bhagwan Das, moved to Delhi from Lahore in the summer of 1947, refugees in their own land. His petty cash only offered a month's sustenance to the large family, but what he didn't have in money, he made up in grit and ambition. He started off what was today an 850 crore empire of steel, with his son carrying on the family legacy, and making it bigger and better than ever. Like in most cases, Rajesh expected his son, Rahul to finish his education and be part of the family business. Yet the youngest Bhatia, for reasons known only to him, wanted to stay away from his family and the colossal bungalow in Delhi where he was born and brought up.

Rahul Bhatia slammed down the pedal of his black Mahindra Scorpio, tucking in his shirt while driving with one hand. He had 15 minutes to get from Aundh to his office in IT park in Hinjewadi, during morning rush hour. The SUV was his first true passion. But, its entire horsepower did not help him in manoeuvring the vehicle through the tight spaces between cars trying to race through one traffic light after another. At another of the multitude crossings, he looked at the digital clock on the traffic light, '90 seconds! Why today? Why today of all days!' Rahul's phone crackled as he started venting his frustration.

'Rahul. Have you reached office or not?' the sharp voice was checking again.

'Nope, just two blocks away. I am stuck at a signal.'

'For once in your life, god damnit, take things seriously. This is supposed to be the most f*****g important day in your career and you are leaving no stones unturned to make it a mess,' Deepak Agnihotri's exasperated voice preached the familiar reprove.

'I know, I know, I was preparing for this interview till late night and couldn't get up on time,' Rahul replied sheepishly, nodding his head.

'Hurry up.'

'Yeah, boss.'

He hung up the phone looking at the seconds left for the traffic signal to change, waiting eagerly to chase his way out. There were three more team members alongside him who had to present to HR their profiles, work accomplished so far and their understanding of their client. The best presentation would get a chance to work for the company onsite. But it wasn't the presentation that made Rahul anxious, he knew he'd hit that on the mark. He was afraid of his own luck, having been betrayed by it on previous occasions.

Rahul parked his car in a rush, grabbed his laptop bag and ran towards the entrance, slinging his ID card around his neck while the guard checked his bag.

He was 15 minutes late. *What if they don't allow me to make the presentation? Is it possible that something would go well? Something always has to go wrong!* His thoughts carried him to the closed door of the conference room, not knowing what to expect once he turned the handle. He took a deep breath, wiped the tip of his shoes against the back of his trousers, swept his hair back and finally entered.

'Phew! It's only you guys! Where is the PM?' Rahul whistled in relief as he saw the occupants of the room.

'He's not here yet,' said one of the other contestants. *What a relief! Agnihotri was losing his shit with me today!*

'He sent a message about delaying the proceedings by half an hour.' said another nervous colleague.

Rahul smiled knowing very well that his boss was helping him by saving him from an embarrassment in front of the HR team. Enthusiastic and determined to make the best of this opportunity, Rahul settled back in his chair and started mentally revising his presentation.

Just then the door opened. 'Hi guys,' Deepak Agnihotri, dressed in a crisp grey business suit walked in along with two senior members from HR. He glanced at Rahul and shook his head indulgently. Rahul was his favourite badass. As much as he admired the younger guy's spontaneity and charm, he disapproved him in equal amount for his carelessness. He believed that out of his four chosen team members Rahul was the most talented and deserving candidate to go to a client abroad and represent their company.

'Guys, we will be calling you one by one. Good luck.' he entered the conference room.

Two Hours Later

Rahul's presentation had gone well. He came out of the conference room smiling. He had the knack of convincing people. His friends credited this knack to a lineage of successful businessmen. Rahul chucked them with a reply, 'Every man born is different from the other, and if my father and grandfather were successful in one direction, I am destined to be successful in something other.'

He reached his desk and while arranging it, his eyes fell upon a photo sitting on one corner. A slow smile spread across his face as he picked up the frame. It was a picture of three good looking young guys, fashioned like mavericks from *Top Gun*. The three of them had their arms on the other's shoulders, standing next to each other, flashing a huge grin towards the camera. Behind them was their old university's red concrete building. Taken a few years ago, it had 'The Clan of GMD' splashed across the top corner and three signatures under the image of the person. To the left was Rahul himself, next to him his two best friends, his brothers—Rehan Khan, on the far right and in the centre, a tall, well-built guy with the looks of a model, stood Ritesh Dhawan.

CHAPTER 2

―⚊―

Bhiwadi, Rajasthan
Monday, 10 October 2011, 7.45 a.m.

Rehan kick started his Hero Honda Splendour. The old bike growled and then died again. It was early in the morning and the bike needed more than couple of kicks to catch. Rehan's ammi made her way to him, walking down the open courtyard of their house. Rehana Khan, the epitome of simplicity, wore a simple blue salwar suit, her head covered with a plain white dupatta. Her slightly wrinkled but smiling face exuded motherly love. Stuffing the tiffin she held, in Rehan's bag she said, 'Son, the money from your father's pension was used in buying the monthly ration. We need to pay for the electricity bill and other expenses. Do you have some money?'

Rehan smiled and opened his wallet only to find two five hundred rupee notes in it. He took out both and handed them to his mother. Rehana smiled, and kept one, putting the other five hundred rupee note back in her son's wallet. 'I will manage with this.' Rehan did not insist his mother to take the money. He knew that she had the ability to survive the toughest conditions for she had bought him up in a similar fashion. He leant in and hugged his mom, his warm brown eyes mirroring hers. As his bike finally started and he rode out, he waved a goodbye to his mother and saw her walking slowly back into the house behind the closed old iron gate.

Rehan, with his neatly parted long black hair, clean shaven oval face and long nose, looked very much the small-town boy. Wearing the factory uniform, a light blue shirt and dark blue trousers, he knocked and entered the air-conditioned cabin of the chairman.

'May I come in, sir?' he said softly. The room smelled of a cheap rose room freshener. Satyendra Chaudhary looked up at him and gave an earnest smile. Mahadev Metal Industries was founded by Satyendra Chaudhary and his two MBA sons in the year 1997. The now five-hundred-employees-strong firm specialized in manufacturing, exporting and trading of exhaust pipes for two wheeler automobiles.

Rehan, a mechanical engineer from the reputed Manav Sanrachna University, was a topper in his batch. He worked as a Design Officer in the firm. Being one of the trusted employees of the company he had quadrupled Rehan up as an Engineer, Design Consultant, Process Supervisor and Shop Floor Manager.

'The designs are ready, sir, please check them and approve before I send them to shop floor,' said Rehan.

Satyendra Chaudhary flashed a smile and signed the documents without reading them. 'Son, you are an asset to my company. There is no need to check what you have already done. I have complete trust in you.' He handed the file back to Rehan. 'Thank you, sir', Rehan smiled.

Anant Dharmadhikari, a contemporary of Mr Chaudhary, was sitting across from him at his desk. They were old friends and fellow industrialists. He looked at Rehan stepping out of the office while carefully closing the door and enquired, 'Why do you trust this boy so much?'

'I know Rehan from childhood. His father Rahim Khan was a clerk at the State Industrial Development Corporation (SIDC) in Bhiwadi. I used to frequent the SIDC office to get clearances for setting up the factory, and Rahim was the nicest and most honest person I had ever met in this world. He helped me genuinely and was instrumental in getting fast approvals. He firmly believed that the fortune of this small town rested in the shoulders of this factory, that it would generate employment for the youth and with people working here and being paid, they would have more money to spend and hence the growth of real estate, good schools, and shopping malls will eventually follow.'

'And it so happened too. With this factory doing well, various other ancillary factories also came alive and now our Bhiwadi is no more a backward village. It's one of the most promising industrial towns in the country,' he continued.

'Rahim Khan, died of blood cancer when Rehan was in college. Rahim's wife is uneducated. She did all the hard work that a mother could do for his son, from teaching cooking to setting up a ladies boutique shop. She did all that was required to provide for Rehan.

'Rehan scored very well in his engineering and he could have got a high-paying job in an MNC and could have flown out of the country along with his mother. But he chose to fulfil his father's dream and came back to work in Bhiwadi. His father was a patriot and believed that the talent of the nation should be used for the development of this country. Rehan is a gem for my company. His hard work, dedication and intelligence has made my company grow multifold. May God bless him,' said an emotional Satyendra Chaudhary.

After winding up his work in the evening, Rehan rode to the Saint Pal Orphanage, his old bike zigzagged through the traffic. He parked his bike just inside the old wrought iron gate. The old building displayed signs of being worn out. The slanted wooden roof was withering off and the paint and cement of the walls were cracked and broken in places. The building was spread in approximately 2,900 sqft area and had three bedrooms and one living room that served as an office and a caretaker's room. The building housed 25 kids of different age groups under its roof. He saw a bunch of children playing in the ground in front of the building. Rehan's eyes were searching for someone.

'Rehan bhaiya,' he heard a cute voice call out.

He turned, his eyes sparkling as he saw little Swapnil waddling towards him wearing a loose white shirt and brown shorts. He picked up the five-year-old and hugged him tight.

'How was the day, kid?'

'It was great Rehan bhaiya, Madam taught us D, E, F,' Swapnil made signs with his little fingers.

'Wow, my boy is so intelligent!' He kissed him on the forehead. Swapnil jumped out of his clutches and ran towards the see-saw where other kids were playing. Rehan had adopted this little boy and it was part of his daily routine to come visit the child and talk to him. He turned towards the office to meet with and share a cup of tea with Sitaram Jetley, manager of the orphanage, fondly called as 'chacha' by one and all.

'I have deposited this month's fee for Swapnil in the orphanage bank account, chacha,' he said to the manager.

Sitaram was engrossed in paperwork, but he looked up and smiled, 'Thank you, Rehan. God bless you. Come sit. The tea is ready.' His thin fingers pointed toward the lone wooden chair in front of the table.

'How are things, Sitaram chacha?'

The fifty-eight-year-old widower with ginger beard and neatly parted grey hair pushed his glasses back on his nose to their position and straightened up his thin frame, 'If it had not been for people like you beta, this place would have fallen apart by now,' his wrinkled eyes shone with gratitude. He was referring to the yearly donation that Rehan would manage to collect from the association of industries in Bhiwadi in the name of this orphanage.

Rehan smiled unpretentiously and sipped his tea. His eyes caught sight of the four new children—three girls and a boy, who looked to be between three to six years of age, sitting in a corner of the room, busy, playing with toys.

'Who are these kids?'

'They are new entrants in the orphanage. Abandoned by their parents.' Sitaram's voice resonated with emotion.

Rehan shook his head, 'Again the same story! Again, children suffer because of their weak parents! Why bother bringing life to this world when they don't have the courage to deal with the outcome? When will this stop? Why can't humans change and stop being so weak willed? When will we have the temerity to stand on our feet and take the world head on?' his frustration at society bursting forth in an unconscious outburst. *When will we have GMD?* A strong voice echoed from the back of his memories.

'Son, people are not born bad. It's how they react to particular situation or problems that make them good or bad.' Sitaram offered the learnings from his experience.

Rehan felt agitated inside. He felt helpless; angst that would erupt like a volcano. Finishing his tea he stepped out of the room. His mind was a jumble of unsaid thoughts. The atrocities that children had to face even today astounded him, depressed and disheartened him. That people still chose to run away from their situation rather than dealing with them, the lack of backbone really got to Rehan. As he neared his home, he pushed these thoughts to the back of his mind. As usual, thinking about things like these brought back bittersweet memories of his two best friends. He pushed away the cobwebs of the past and parked his bike to the side of the courtyard. The old traditional house had three small rooms and a kitchen built around an open central courtyard. Originally a vibrant colour, the green had now faded to a light grassy hue. Enveloped in the scent of incense sticks, his ammi's signature deal, he washed up and changed to freshly laundered kurta pyjamas.

He coiled his lean frame down in front of the TV and picked up the remote as his ammi served him his dinner. He had barely started on the steaming hot tadka daal when she held his arm and pointed at the news flash. Rehan's heart filled with dread as he saw the news of the attack by NIA team on a group of terrorists in Karol Bagh and that the leader Major Ritesh Dhawan had been seriously injured in the exercise. His heart beat fast, he was torn between pride for what Ritesh had accomplished and concern for his best friend's well-being. With trembling hands, he did the only thing he could think of…he picked up his phone and dialled a number.

Rahul was at the wheel, driving back home that evening, characteristically swinging a cigarette to and fro his lips, a force of habit while he exuded tension. The ringing of his cell phone brought him out of his contemplation as he saw Rehan's name flash on the screen. A huge smile, his first genuine smile of the day ran across his face.

'*Bhai jaan ko salaam*, so finally you get time to call me!' exclaimed Rahul with surprise. A plethora of emotions ranging from happy to shock to sombre flashed across his face as he listened to his friend's voice. Rehan wasted no time in relaying the news about Ritesh. He was after all more than a friend to them, he was their brother, a third of their trio.

'I'll be on the next flight to Delhi.'

—⚬—

Rehan was packing his bag. Keeping up a steady stream of tears, he had decided on taking the next passenger train from Bhiwadi to Delhi. Well aware of Ritesh's risky career choice made this an expected situation but dealing with it in reality was a lot harder for Rehan. *He will beat death. He is a born fighter. I know him.*

He felt his ammi's hand on his back and turning around wrapped himself in the comfort of her embrace. She understood her son's angst. Ritesh was more or less a second son to her. She too wanted to cry, but held strong for Rehan. She stroked his back soothingly and said, 'Ritesh will be fine. Here, take this taweez. I had got it from the Ajmer Dargah for him last time. Tie it on his hand. I will pray to Allah to make my son healthy and fit again.'

Rehan dried his eyes, put the taweez inside a pocket in the bag and headed towards the railway station.

The cool October breeze ruffled Rehan's hair as he sat staring out of the second class general coach. He barely registered the noise and chatter inside the compartment. Sitting by the window seat, his eyes were focused on two young guys riding their bikes close to each other yet fast, racing with the train at night. His mind transported him to three boys from a different time, riding their bikes against the wind.

CHAPTER 3

―᠅―

Six Years Ago, 2005
National Highway No. 8 (NH8)

The early morning sun was bright and was reflecting off the rim of the blue Bajaj Pulsar 180cc bike, riding ahead of the black Royal Enfield Thunderbird. The lead was not sustained for long; the 346cc and 19.5bhp engine of the Thunderbird with a decisive shift of gears and with a rambunctious roar raced past Pulsar.

Rehan, riding pillion behind Ritesh was on the Pulsar. Rahul, driving the monster that roared past all and sundry, was acting out a bet between the three as to who would reach the university first.

Inseparable from their first semester at their engineering college, Ritesh pursuing Computers, Rehan Mechanical and Rahul Electronics, met in their common hostel and considered themselves more than friends and companions. They were brothers from separate mothers. Today was the start of their seventh semester, their final year and they were driving back from Bhiwadi, Rehan's hometown, after spending the last week of their vacations there. Basking in the early summer countryside, the sunny meadows near Rehan's home, the rustic charm of an old city and fervour of a growing town, it was a gratifying experience for even the metropolitan Rahul and familiar to Ritesh. They loved the warmth of ammi's hospitality and the home-cooked desi ghee delectable dishes that they feasted on. It had become a ritual in the last three years to rejuvenate there after the gruelling semesters at college.

The Gurgaon-Faridabad road led to the prestigious Manav Sanrachna University, one of the largest and oldest private universities that offered engineering, dental and even fine arts courses—attracting a young diverse crowd from Delhi and the surrounding cities. The two bikes and their riders, riding against time, aimed to make it back to the university in time for the induction ceremony for the new additions, their juniors, fuchchas. The boys didn't want to miss checking out the new girls that would join their college and calling their dibs. It was imperative that they know which fresh face belonged to which class.

The Thunderbird growled frantically as Rahul pumped the accelerator to full throttle and took a steep cut on Ritesh's left, gunning for the two wheeler section of the toll booth.

Ritesh laughed, 'Dog!' As he steadied his Pulsar again, he shouted above the wind, to Rehan, 'He'll have to stop at the toll, we will catch up with him then.' Rehan nodded in affirmation.

Just when they expected Rahul to stop at the toll gate, they saw him taking his bike off the road, riding over a small mound of hard surface that circumvented the toll gate. The Thunderbird emanated smoke from its exhaust pipe and roared as Rahul pushed it upwards, defying gravity. They watched as he perfectly executed a three-foot leap from the edge of the mound, back on to the road on the other side of the toll booth, the shockers of the Thunderbird absorbing the impact, as Rahul pumped his hand to the air, in victory.

'Royal bastard, he is.' Ritesh shook his head and followed the same route.

Rahul was leading the race, his eyes glued to the road and alert. He sensed a car overtaking him.

He whistled softly as he saw a sleek chauffer-driven black Audi driving next to him. But more than the new car, it was the passenger in it that intrigued him. In the back seat was a girl looking out of the open window. Her face was raised to the sky, eyes closed, and the wind in her hair. Her fingers extended out making waves in the wind. The delicate bracelet on her wrist, glinted, the sun reflecting off the diamonds in it. She laughed as the wind blew back her feather earrings, her face breaking into the most beautiful expression. As the car crossed him by, she opened her eyes and looked straight at him. Her warm brown eyes full of laughter blinked at him as the car overtook him.

In an instant, Rahul felt hooked. This stranger, whose name he didn't know, whose voice he hadn't heard, because of whom, for some reason, he could hear his heart beat, slower and then suddenly very fast, left him with a smile on his face.

Rahul's momentary distraction allowed Ritesh to catch up and overtake him. Rehan turned around to give Rahul a playful taunt on his loss and was stunned to see him smiling vaguely.

Rehan sniggered and signalled to Ritesh with his right fist to keep going as they could possibly now win the race, their destination wasn't far. The blue Pulsar kept the momentum for a few seconds before a loud roar behind them signalled that Rahul was back in the game. They looked on in wonder at the bike racing past them, Rahul's face staring steadfastly ahead, focused and driven. He seemed to be following the Audi, swerving between cars unnecessarily. *I have to find out who this girl is; chase her...get to know her!*

Rahul prayed fervently as he guided his bike behind the Audi. The car took a left turn, onto a by lane. Rahul, only a few metres behind, followed. As he was turning, a herd of buffaloes came rushing out on to the narrow lane. There was a loud screech as Rahul applied the brakes and swung the bike to his right. Pumping the accelerator again, he tried catching up with the car, overtaking the last of the buffaloes from the corner. He had just managed to cross the herd, when he saw a black tempo-truck coming down the wrong side of the road, straight at him. All Rahul saw before swerving off the road again was a huge, menacing evil eye symbol drawn on the front grill of the truck, the speed causing him to lose his balance and control over the heavy bike. The tyres were digging into the loose gravel and dirt path, and spraying up bits of stone. He braked hard, the bike's gravity shifted and it toppled over, as the truck rushed past.

Behind the bushes, a pair of distinctive amber eyes looked up in alarm. *There isn't supposed to be anyone here. No one will know what I am doing.* With a disfigured left hand, this man wiped his brow, four thick fingers in left hand with no index finger, while his unique wolf eyes tried to see who caused the commotion. He slid his right hand into the lower pockets of his cargo pants and brought out a small knife. Taking measured steps, he walked towards the noise.

As he crossed over the rough bushes, he saw a man lying face down a few hundred feet away. Hunched, he moved fast towards him, his knife held tightly to the side, observing his surroundings. As he neared the site of the crash, he saw the man was pinned under the heavy bike. He was lying face down, but there didn't seem to be any blood. He walked slowly towards this man's head to check if he was alive. As he bent down, he heard a shout.

'Jackal!'

'Dr Jackal' looked up and saw Ritesh and Rehan putting their bike on the stand and running towards him. He immediately got up and looking at them said, 'Fellas, who is he? Oh wait... I take it, this one is Rahul?'

'Genius, doctor! Help, now!' Rehan urged as he lifted the bike off Rahul's leg.

Ritesh went down on his knees and gingerly lifted Rahul's head on to his lap, asking if he was okay. Rahul nodded and opened his eyes and coughed out the dirt, wiping his face with his hand. Rehan and Jackal had meanwhile straightened the bike.

'Take it easy, Rahul. Is anything broken?' Ritesh asked.

'Are you hurt?' inquired Rehan. Rahul shook his head. 'The knee cap and gear saved me from any injury.'

'Lucky, you didn't hit your head, get up and move now,' Jackal said in a mocking tone.

The three boys looked at him and asked in a surprised chorus, 'What are you doing here?'

'Research,' Dr Jackal responded with a straight face.

They looked at him sceptically.

'It's none of your business actually; I heard a crashing sound and came out to check.' Jackal added as he stalked off towards the forest behind the bushes.

Jai Kishan Amre was fondly nicknamed 'Dr Jackal' by his college mates. Like most sharp and brilliant minds, he too was a loner. He was the illegitimate son of a rich father, who had long since taken him off the social and family circles but would send him money, enough to pay for his college and other needs. He was a Biochemical Engineer and more often than not indulged in his 'research'. No one knew what it was, or what it was for.

The boys helped Rahul up, dusting off his leather jacket. All three donned their helmets this time, which were locked onto the bikes. Rahul sat behind Rehan who would drive his bike the remainder of the way to college.

Later the three boys were sitting in their usual spot in the college canteen, three bottles of Thums Up in front of them.

Rahul, leaning his chair back ran his hands through his hair as he sipped this fizzy drink.

'Didn't know you had Valentino Rossi in you!' said Ritesh sarcastically.

As they both looked at Rahul, his expression turned sheepish, he said, 'I saw someone in the car.'

'Someone? As in, a girl?' asked Rehan.

'Yeah.'

'And you like an ass tried to follow her?'

'Yes.'

'Have you gone nuts, saale? You could have died! Driving like an idiot, not seeing where you're going and that too without a helmet!'

Rahul did not respond to Ritesh. He took out a slightly crushed pack of Marlboro from his Calvin Klein jeans pocket and lit one cigarette with his customised Zippo lighter.

'Was she so special?' asked Rehan.

Rahul raised his shoulders nonchalantly while taking a drag.

Rehan grinned, 'Don't worry, if she is destined to be in your life you will meet her again, bhai.'

Rahul smirked and made ringlets out of the smoke blowing from his mouth.

'What is it with you and smoking nowadays? It's increasing day by day. Throw it out, or you'll die before me!' Ritesh plucked the cigarette from Rahul's lips and put it out, crushing it under his foot.

Rahul stammered his disapproval while Rehan sniggered looking at the cafeteria clock.

'OH SHIT, we are late for the newcomers induction. Bhaago!' All three pushed their chairs back and sprinted towards the auditorium.

Watching them run, the boys on the far end of the canteen also understood the reason of the rush and proclaimed, 'OH SHIT' and ran after them.

When they crossed the gate of the canteen, a couple of their batchmates saw the rush towards the auditorium and immediately understood the reason for their urgency, 'OH SHIT', they too chorused and ran after them.

They crossed the main lobby and were running up the stairs when a few other boys saw them and slapped their heads, 'OH SHIT', and followed them towards the main auditorium hall.

Jackal was relieving himself in the boy's toilet, adjacent to the stairs, when he heard the thundering footsteps. He also realized the urgency and in the hurry of zipping up, his zipper got caught with his vital organ. He cried out, 'OH SHIT.'

Rehan, Rahul and Ritesh were the first to enter the large induction hall to a resounding chorus of 'Good morning'. They slipped in quietly, trying to be inconspicuous and found separate seats for themselves among the crowd.

Ms Lalita Verma aka Lilli, as she was fondly nicknamed by the students, was welcoming the new joinees. The new boys whistled appreciatively as Ms Lilli smiled down at all of them.

Like Sushmita Sen from the movie *Main Hoon Na*, Ms Lilli, too was someone everyone desired after. The boys wanted her, girls wanted to be like her. In her '30s, she looked 10 years younger. Her curvaceous and well-endowed svelte figure was always draped in a slinky chiffon sari; she had everyone in the university, from the old fuddy-duddy lecturers to the peaky young boys, lusting after her. The gossip was that she was single and loved the attention. A lot of resident boys had signed up for her yoga sessions early in the morning, the attraction seemingly evident. It was rumoured that every semester, there were at least three anonymous proposal letters daily, pushed into her locker outside the staff room.

As she stood on the stage, setting up her laptop to the projector, there seemed to be a collective sigh travel across the room.

Rahul and Rehan quickly glanced at Ritesh with teasing looks. The grapevine was that Ms Lilli only had eyes for Ritesh and was rather fond of him. This was one thing he was teased mercilessly about. Ritesh, who was a seedha guy when it came to respecting his professors, went red in the face every time this was brought up.

As the presentation started, Ms Lilli started talking about the architecture of this grand old college, and its history and facilities. All the senior boys quickly sat up straight and ogled at the fresh faces of the girls in the hall.

Dr Jackal also waddled his way into the auditorium. He identified a space beside a girl and as he sat down she was startled, his amber eyes scaring her. Without any haste she got up and changed her seat. Ms Lilli was in the middle of her presentation when she noticed the commotion.

As she continued with her speech, her eyes roamed the hall, looking for the culprits. She noticed one of them among a few boys sitting very attentively at the back as Ritesh. *I could recognize him anywhere. But, this is extremely annoying.*

Ritesh looked up and realized they had been caught; he shifted lower in his seat and avoided eye contact with Ms Lilli.

'You, the boy in blue shirt,' she said. There was suddenly a pin drop silence. Ritesh too kept quiet.

'Come on, I know and you know I'm talking to you. Now please do me the courtesy and get up. Don't make me come down there.'

Ritesh kept his head down for a second, before he realized that everyone in the auditorium was staring at him.

He pushed his hair back and with a sheepish smile he looked up and stood. All the girls in the room gasped as they noticed his 6.2 feet tall frame, slightly muscular body, devilishly cute face and long hair.

'Mr Dhawan, good of you to join us. Did I miss the memo? Have you been demoted?' Ms Lilli asked in her seductive sultry voice. 'You are a final year student, if I recall correctly? Have you come to share your experiences with the new students?' she enquired sarcastically, crossing her arms across her front.

'I...ah, mistook this as one of my lectures, ma'am,' Ritesh said, while trying to keep a straight face.

'You can't be alone, two of your other monkey friends will also be here. Get up sweeties, before I call the Dean,' she challenged the others.

Rehan and Rahul also got up slowly, one contrite and the other nonchalant respectively. She smiled and shook her head.

'Come, come be my guest,' she gestured them to come to the stage.

They looked at each other and slowly walked down towards her. Their other batchmates were trying to catch their eye and plead with them to not say anything. Ms Lilli, with her sharp eyes noticed these furtive actions and said, 'All the third year boys, and I mean all of you still hiding amongst your first years, will come up to the stage, now!'

Roughly a dozen boys stood up from their various positions across the room.

Ms Lilli rolled her eyes and pointed them all up on stage. A scattering of nervous laughter broke in the auditorium. The fresh faces were scared, as they didn't know what might happen to those that broke the rules.

Ritesh, Rahul and Rehan were waiting on the stage for their batchmates. Ms Lilli stood in front of them, her back facing the crowd and said softly, 'Quite the little ringleaders, aren't we? Rules, sweeties, rules are not meant to be broken. Wait for it.'

'Ah! Now that all your seniors have shown you just how juvenile they are, let's figure out a punishment for them?'

Rehan, trying to be a peacemaker, apologized to Ms Lilli, 'We're extremely sorry, ma'am. We won't do it again.'

'Enough, Mr Khan. You know as well as I do, you will continue doing this till you graduate. The Dean will deal with all of you, but in the meantime, you all, yes, all 15 of you will pose like chickens on the side of the stage and hold your ears till my session is finished. Since you have all acted like naughty children, you will be dealt like them too. Now hurry up,' she said as the crowd behind her started laughing softly.

The boys all lowered their eyes and went to stand by the sides of the stage.

As Rahul lowered himself, he heard someone giggle. He turned his head towards the side of the voice and his heart flipped. *She is here! She joined our university!*

Rahul, sitting in a chicken position and holding his ears, couldn't hear Ms Lalita continuing with the presentation, specifically pointing out the ramifications of being undisciplined. As the blood rushed to his head, all he could concentrate on was this beautiful, petite girl sitting in the front row, trying to control her laughter, as the diamond bracelet reflected the auditorium lights.

CHAPTER 4

The slightly sombre mood in the college canteen later that morning was credited to the seniors that got caught. Not only were they punished as they were, but the Dean too had a go at them on the first day itself. But their mood wasn't going to be kept down for long...there was anticipation in the air. By lunch break, all the seniors would have regrouped and recuperated, ready for their 'officially unofficial' introduction to their juniors.

Rehan, Rahul and Ritesh were the three leaders of the pack of hostellers. There was an eternal animosity between the hostellers and day scholars, with each group thinking they had the sweeter deal. They fancied themselves to be like the mutants of Professor X and Magneto—both groups having historically tightened their stands against each other. Such was the intensity of their emotions, that whenever the lights went out in the class or during the changeover time between one professor leaving and other one coming in to the class, a hosteller or a day scholar wouldn't miss the chance of hurling an abuse in anonymity toward the rival pack.

The day scholars pack was headed by Pankaj Bhoj aka Pankaj 'bhaiya' as he was reverentially called. Out of bhaiya ji's many achievements, the biggest was his duration of stay at the university. He had the distinction of remaining in the final year of engineering for the longest since its inception! For the past four years he had been a constant father figure in the Civil Engineering class. Rumour was that he was serving out the tadipaar (banishment) notice issued to him by the UP Police. To any new comer, Pankaj bhaiya's cronies would boast of his lineage—four elder brothers who were shot dead, murdered one by one in a deadly gang war somewhere in western UP. He claimed to have broken the bones of one of his brother's slayer and since then had found a perfect hiding place as a student in the university. Nobody dared question the authenticity of his story. Several of his exams were extended post the 'mercy' attempts, the term denoted for the fourth attempt to clear an exam. Pankaj bhaiya was also an active member of the Student Union of India (SUI) and ran his parallel dominion in the Day Scholar world.

There was a custom in the university, one that was upheld mightier than any other rule; a day scholar fresher could not give his or her 'formal introduction' to hostellers first and day scholars seniors second, and vice versa too. The repercussions were severe.

But today, bhaiya ji wasn't back in college yet, and therefore, the juniors had no choice, but to report to the hostellers, much to the dismay of the day scholar seniors, who without a leader present couldn't instigate a fight.

Later That Afternoon

All the freshers shuffled into the large air-conditioned section of the canteen. The hostel seniors according to their ranks— immediate, super or supreme seniors, had taken up various positions around the hall. The supreme seniors, Rahul, Ritesh and Rehan's batch were sitting on tables at the far end, on what they referred to as the head table, overlooking the proceedings. The juniors were split into groups of eight each and made to sit around the round tables placed strategically facing the head table, each manned by a senior couple.

Strict instructions regarding the prohibition of physical and verbal abuse had been dished out to all the seniors in advance, abiding by the laws of the university. This was to be a hands-off, communication-only session.

Sania, a supreme senior, was put in charge of managing the entire event. She came from the Jatt-lands and while she looked slender, was strong as an ox, with a voice and personality to match. She had wielded her deceptive looks quite often against the day scholars over the years, and left them beaten to a pulp. Today, she was the spokesperson on behalf of three years of seniors. She climbed on to a table and shouted, 'Hey!'

The canteen quietened down and looked at her with rapt attention.

'All the day scholars and hostllers, you will be asked to sing and dance, recite filmi dialogues as part of your introduction to all the seniors. For all the hostllers, there is a custom in our college. We give you chance to be free from the ragging if you come clear on the tests.'

A sigh of relief and excitement floated among the junior crowd.

Sania smiled and continued, 'On the basis of your performance in the fun round which includes singing, dancing and emoting film stars, qualifiers would be selected to appear in either the Annual Red Bull contest or The Annual Blue Bull contest. This is a two way check: one—fun, two—power and control of an individual.' She counted off, holding one finger up after another.

A murmur burst open in the small crowd. The hostel students looked with disdain at their day scholar counterparts as their seniors had presented them the chance to be declared free from ragging.

Sania clapped to draw the attention of the crowd towards her. 'So, the hostllers, as you know, the prize at the end of it is immunity from ragging for the entire year. It also means you get to be one of us. You get to sit, eat, enjoy with us. You get to have your batchmate do all your homework for an entire year, if you want. No senior will take your lunch money; no one will make you run around doing their work. Full freedom. Got it?' she ended to a sudden burst of chattering amongst the freshers.

The seniors went to their designated respective tables to start the round of introductions, as Rahul got up and started looking around the room. Rehan looked at him and wondered out loud, 'What's got into your pants?'

Over the sound of Ritesh laughing, Rahul said, 'She's here yaar...' in a dreamy, misty tone. Rehan too stood up to see this source of Rahul's agony and pleasure, 'Kahan? Junior?'

Rahul spotted his girl, sitting halfway away from him, in a stroke of luck on a table being manned by Sania. He whistled, and called out to her to join them. He mock dusted off his leather jacket and ran his hand thru his gelled hair in the time it took Sania to reach him.

'What?'

'I need info on that girl in your group. The girl in red. Everything you've got and more,' he nodded towards the table and the girl of his dreams.

Sania turned around to look at the girl Rahul was pointing out.

She raised her eyebrows and remarked, 'Are you in love, Mr Bhatia?'

'He is very quick, huh?' she inquired from Ritesh and Rehan.

Rahul puts his arm around her and pulls her close, 'Chal na! You can do this for me. You love me. Like I love you. Jaa! I'm waiting.'

Shaking her head and laughing she walked back to her table and raised her middle finger at Rahul.

Rahul waited with bated breath. *This is true love, believe me.*

Sania came back after 20 minutes, 'Her name is Neha Khare, daughter of a famous child specialist in Delhi. She's joined Electronics, day scholar.

'Electronics! What!...same branch. Awesome! God! I will help her...' Rahul exclaimed.

'Oh puhleez, help yourself first... You have barely scraped through passing marks in your last exam,' laughed Sania.

'Anyway, her favourite actor is the Edward Cullen guy; she loves *Maroon* 5 and loves hanging out in Khan Market. I have taken her phone number and will pass it on to you. Happy?'

'Wow Sani, *tusi great ho paaji!*' Rahul hugged her and bent down to kiss her head.

'Sania! Don't call me Sani, jerk! You owe me, big time.' She said as she ran out from under Rahul's playful grasp. *'Kiss mat kariyo. Disease ho jayegi mereko.'*

Ritesh clapped Rahul on his back, 'What luck, saale... Lover boy! He's so failing this year.'

After five minutes of playful banter amongst the three best friends, Rahul got up and went to the table where Neha sat. His imposing height and good looks, with his leather jacket and expensive jeans were an add-on to his Delhi-boy personality. The surrounding tables became quieter as Rahul passed by. He was used to it. People stared. He had typical bad boy looks, a strong jaw, straight nose, fair and longish gelled hair.

When he reached Neha's table, the girls seemed to have frozen in their places, barely breathing. It was only Neha who was looking away; on purpose apparently, her chin in the air. He knew how this game was played. He stood there looking at her, without saying a word, till all the other group members looked at her too and she had no choice but to look back at Rahul. *What the hell is going on? Who is this guy?*

'Come.'

Neha looked at Sania, who gestured her to leave with Rahul. She got up timidly, and smoothed her skirt down and picked up her bag. Rahul waited for her and gestured for her to walk with him.

The entire canteen's eyes were on them as they approached the head table. Rahul pulled out a chair for Neha, picked up a Thums Up can from the centre of the table and offered one to her. Rehan and Ritesh were cradling their own cans of Thums Up. Rahul sat on the table and asked her to sit. With one foot on the chair to the side, he opened the can.

'This is Rahul. *Naam to suna hoga*,' said Ritesh in a mocking tone and a wink.

Surprised at the clichéd Bollywood dialogue, Neha turned towards Ritesh and smiled, 'Quite old...no?'

She looked up and saw Rahul, smiling at her. She was busy contemplating whether to return his smile, when Rahul started, 'That's Ritesh, Rehan and I'm...well, you know me,' nodding towards the guys.

'I'm in the seventh semester of Electronics Engineering. You can come to me for any assistance—books, viva preparations, anybody teasing you, just let me know,' Rahul took a sip of his Thums Up, trying to be all cool.

'Are you saying that you want to be my godfather?' Neha sipped her Thums Up, crossed her legs gracefully and smiled back at him innocently, but with a mischievous look in her eyes.

She caught Rahul off guard. Before he could reply, Neha got up, 'You think of the answer and let me know, "sir". Thanks for the drink.' She strutted back to her table and left Rahul with his mouth hanging open. *An attitude to match. What an amazing chick!*

Later That Night

In an 'under construction' section of the old boys hostel, sat a group of nervous freshers. Who were selected on the basis of their performance in the fun test. Stage Two of the ragging fest, 'The Blue Bull', was about to begin.

The entire ragging process was termed 'The Bull Tests', a series of prestigious competitions that would result in the winning juniors being awarded the titles of 'The Blue Bull' and 'The Red Bull' each.

The Blue Bull was an underground honour given to those who had proven their articulation and imaginative skills. The Blue Bull competition began with all the students queuing up and choosing their favourite celebrities. They then had to articulate why said celebrity was their favourite. Without being told the point of the questioning, the students came up with celebrities from the obvious—movies, TV, theatre, etc., but it became fun when they chose politicians or professors to gain points. The next question always was a hypothetical one—describe with full detail, vividness, and action, emotions, and voice modulations, your first and only night of intimacy with the chosen celebrity. What follows is a few hours of an endless rolling-on-the-floor laughter session. Quite a few, at this stage bow out in defeat and a daring few take on the challenge. Those who succeeded in tantalizing the seniors with their articulation and elaborate description of the imaginary whoopee, were further invited by the seniors in the hostel during night to share the dais with them in the ultimate test of control of emotions. The winner was given the title of the Mr Blue Bull and was awarded exemption from ragging.

Rahul, along with a few other batchmates led the juniors towards Stage Three.

Rehan and Ritesh along with a few other batchmates were standing in the shadows of the old garage area, surrounded by a bunch of selected fresh first years. The guards manning this spot had been given a couple of bottle of rum to keep them happy and at bay.

They were about to lead a fight for title of Mr Red Bull, awarded to him who showed the highest endurance.

The Red Bull competition was for those juniors that believed in 'brawn is might', the guys that had egos taller than their frames. Stage Two of the Red Bull Competition involved the freshers sharing the dais with their seniors, gulping down one beer after another. When the inebriation levels were at their highest those who survived and had guts to take on the challenge further, were made to race one another on a bicycle. The 10km track inside the huge university campus, which was located in the picturesque Aravalli hills, suited their purpose perfectly. Stage Three of the Red Bull Competition was called 'Race-de-Campus' and the winning drunkard cyclist was given the title of the Red Bull and was awarded exemption from ragging. Stories of his escapades would be touted over the years to come.

The Blue Bull Contest, Final Stage, Fortitude Test

Ten juniors had made to the final list; they followed Rahul into the designated dorm room. A digital projector from the college lab had been smuggled in to the dormitory. The laptop was ready, hundred per cent charged.

All the shortlisted kids were seated in a semicircle, facing the screen. The boys were made to strip down to their T-shirts and boxers, nothing more, nothing less. Rahul addressed the gathering, 'Guys, congratulations on making it to Stage Three of the Blue Bulls. This round will check the ultimate staying power and fortitude in you. And the one who will pass this will be awarded the title and will be exempt from ragging.'

'I won the contest three years ago, and trust me; the respect carries on with you when you leave college. You leave behind a legacy.' Rahul flashed them a cocky smile.

Rahul held up a CD case, 'Boys, we have chosen the best of those available. These CDs contain the best blue films you can find anywhere. We will now project the film and it will run for next 45 minutes. We'll be keeping an eye on you as you watch the film together but remember your win lies in *not* getting excited. If you get excited or visibly turned on, you will be kicked out. You will have lost. Remember the key to winning, "that the soft should not get hard!"'

The Red Bull Contest, Final Stage Race-de-Campus, Endurance Test

The other set of selected toughies were standing in a row with cycles that were made available for students by the university to travel inside the huge campus that was sprawled across the big hill. These cycles were borrowed from the campus transport facility. Ritesh stood in front of them, swaying slightly and with red eyes. He was six bottles of 'super strong' beer down, and with a faint lisp, he instructed the fuchchas, 'Nobody will try any unfair means to win the race, no pushing, and no fighting while riding. You ride hard, you ride safe. Mark the words of a Red Bull himself from three years ago, yours truly.' his proud voice boomed. He swung his leg over his bike and then balancing himself stood upright. *Almost four litres of beer down. Phew.*

The whistle signalled the start of the race. The drunken cyclists tried hard to focus on moving their bikes forward. The dim light emanating from the lamp posts alongside the track made the path ahead in darkness tougher still. The 10-metre wide non-cemented track was octagonal and involved a 250 metre climb up a small hill, passing through the main entrance and ending at the boys' hostel.

Jackal played the CD and hit the lights. Additional laptop speakers gave an ambient sound to the room. Ten pairs of curious eyes were glued to the screen. There were 'oohs' from the audience when the goddess of all things x-rated appeared, in nothing but her tiny, sheer bathrobe.

The 12 cyclists were riding hard. There were three riders in the lead, the rest following, each one marginally behind the other, their desire to prove their mettle urging them on. Ritesh and Rehan along with their classmates rode on the bike as marshals and as the first sharp turn came up, there was a unanimous 'oohs' from the cyclists.

Sultry Minny's curves were unrivalled in the industry. Young, eager eyes followed her every move, down every curve, where she wanted them to. Rahul and his friends along with Jackal were focusing on the audience, checking for signs of tumescence. Their eyes were glued on any suspicious movement made by the audience.

At this point of night, the curves of the track seemed sharp. The young beavers in an attempt to prove their worth followed them as commanded. The riders' eyes were focused on the track ahead and Rehan's eyes were peeled for any suspicious movement or unfair play made by the riders.

The male lead was succumbing to sultry Minny's advances, seeing her step into the shower after him. All he wanted was to give her what she wanted. He holds on to her, in an attempt to get started as she moans, 'Conquer me.'

'Sir, may I go to the bathroom?' enquired a boy from the group. *Three minutes.* Rahul and his friends had been waiting for someone to crack down. After all it was not easy to stay unaffected when sultry Minny was doing her thing. The seniors laughed and let him go.

—∞—

The hill was in front of the cyclists and they began their ascent to the top to conquer the height. The fastest rider was the first to buckle down. He began panting and slowed down considerably. The others rode past him. The slowest rider turned out to be strongest and climbed with grit. One of the riders stopped and got down from the cycle. 'Sir, I accept my defeat. I can't ride any further. I am dead.' Ritesh and his friends laughed and let him go.

—∞—

The two leads were moaning in ecstasy. The breathing in the room had reached a hard low pitch. The visuals and sounds from the movie were rising in tempo, aiming for the first climax. Rahul and the team, also getting distracted understood that this was when the boys would react, would falter. Rahul walked back and forth, keeping a close eye on the bunch, all of them as mandated, with their legs apart and hands folded on their chests.

They were waiting for Minny's euphoric cry of ultimate pleasure, when instead, they heard a whimper from within the audience. The seniors heard it loud and clear. *Who was that?*

—∞—

The riders were all racing down the hill. The descent had an essence of ecstasy in it. Cool breeze flew past the riders. The adrenaline rush kicking in. The head light from Ritesh's bike acted as an additional guide for the riders following him in the dark. The near silence of the night was broken by the clatter of crash. *Who was that?*

The junior sitting close to the centre of the semicircle sniffed. He looked to his left and to his right. *I can smell seminal fluid.* He looked behind him and saw Jackal standing there. His eyes flickered invariably to Jackal's pants and he noticed a damp stain on the front of his pants. He sniggered and elbowed his friend to take a look at Jackal's pants. The friend also smirked. Rahul noticed the giggle and saw Jackal making a failed attempt to hide the dampness in his pants. He cursed Jackal for letting the seniors down. Before anyone could react Jackal rushed towards the bathroom.

Ritesh came to a halt with a screech. He along with Rehan ran towards the heap on the stone path. He saw a rider lying down unconscious on the track. His fingers touched the dampness on his clothes. Sweat, puke and something more; the sticky metallic *scent of blood, vital fluid.* With Rehan's help, he picked up the unconscious fresher and rushed towards the medical room.

CHAPTER 5

All India Institute of Medical Sciences, New Delhi
10 October 2011

The siren of the ambulance ripped through the usual cacophony of noises on the Ring Road. In the ambulance rushing towards AIIMS, Ritesh's broken body lay motionless, hooked onto various life support machines. Vikram, willing the ambulance to go faster, held Ritesh's bloody hand in his own fervently praying for his mentor, his friend, his brother and partner to overcome his injuries. *You have to make it, brother.*

At the hospital, senior doctors were waiting for the ambulance to arrive. The calls had come in from the higher ups. This was about the NIA and its finest man. The hospital was about to be overcome with senior officials from the Police, NIA, and the Defence Ministry, possibly even the media.

Vikram looked on as they rushed the stretcher inside; his friend's wounded, none the less large frame making the stretcher seem fragile.

Four Hours Later

Ritesh's parents came running into the ICU ward. They had caught the first flight out of Amritsar after hearing the horrifying news. Vikram had just returned from the conference centre of the hospital, from his debriefing session with Director General Sinha to find that the doctors were still working on Ritesh.

He immediately recognized Mr Dhawan Senior, who looked like an elder replica of his son, tall and strong frame, albeit with a moustache. The lady accompanying him was Mrs Dhawan; soft, yet with the same countenance as Ritesh. Looking into her eyes was like looking at Ritesh's.

He stood to welcome them, 'Good evening, sir, I am Lt Vikram Sharma. I'm part of...'

He was interrupted by Mr Dhawan, 'I know son, Ritesh often talked about all of you. How is he? Where is he?'

'I... ah... He's still in the ICU, sir. They have the best doctors working on him. We got him here as fast as we could,' Vikram replied with a crack in his voice.

He watched as Ritesh's mother moaned quietly. His father quickly turned to support her and pulled her towards the chairs, chanting and repeating, 'He'll be fine. He's strong. He's a fighter. Don't lose hope. He won't like it.'

Vikram saw them and wondered if Mr Dhawan was consoling his wife or asserting it to himself. He quickly sent a text to the director, informing him of Ritesh's parents' arrival, as ordered.

Pune Airport
10 October 2011, 8.30 p.m.

The taxi screeched to a halt and Rahul jumped out of it carrying a leather holdall that his manservant had hurriedly packed up. He handed a thousand rupee note to the cab driver, and shouted, 'Keep the change,' as he ran towards the departure section of the airport.

―⁂―

Six Years Ago, 2005

Rahul sprinted across the corridor chasing Jackal who ran witlessly, trying to save his ass from getting kicked.

'Stop you a**hole. Bloody leak!' Rahul yelled as Jackal disappeared among some kids coming out of their classrooms for the first break.

It was not much later that Rahul caught Jackal. He held him by his collar; Jackal's thin frame trembled under Rahul's grip, 'You ruined the seniors' reputation in front of those greenhorns yesterday.'

Rehan and one of their batchmates, Himanshu, also joined Rahul. Rehan said, 'Kamine, ek toh you have spoiled the name of legendary Dr Jackal, the Shaktiman villain, after whom we nicknamed you, but upar se, the toughness and resiliency that we the hostellers of MSU preach and live by is also gone.'

There was a rare accusation in his voice. Dr Jackal's amber eyes filled up. He looked at his batchmates one by one and saw anguish in them. He could not take this insult any further.

Jai Kishan Amre, aka Dr Jackal, was a genius. With an IQ of 130, he had always been an exceptional child, discussing radical ideas and thoughts with his teachers. As a child, he would solve mathematics sums using the Vedic methods. Yet he was ridiculed and laughed at for his unconventional ideas and mannerisms. His physical appearance didn't help him either. Being born 'different,' with a hairless body and only four fingers on left hand, he lived a secluded childhood. He never complained about the abuse and mockery he received from his companions while growing up, he realized they just didn't understand. He loved and adored the character of Dr Jackal from the famous television serial *Shaktiman*. Dr Jackal starts out as a brilliant scientist but after being ridiculed for his novel ways by the society, he succumbs to the 'dark' powers of another fictional character Tamraj Kilvish, the king of darkness.

Jai Kishan Amre also succumbed to the new-found loneliness and kept himself engrossed in solitary seclusion. Nobody knew what he did and where he went. He lived the life of an intrinsic loner; at first, only attending his classes and then closeting himself up in his dorm room. Rahul met him in the hostel. He empathized with him and included him as an extended member of their gang. With all his genius worth, Dr Jackal was an active contributor to all their mischief.

'Give me a chance at redemption,' pleaded Jackal, bending down on one knee, face down and both hands up in the air, palms facing the roof.

Oh the theatrics, Rahul and Rehan exchanged a smirk.

'Okay, I will give you one chance to do that,' announced Rahul. 'You'll have to do what I say, no questions asked. There is a girl, Neha, in first year, Electronics Engineering. I like her very much and want to impress her. This weekend you will help me do that.'

'Your wish is my command,' Jackal replied.

Nehru Park, New Delhi

In the early hours of dawn, the nip in the air carried a sweet woodsy smell. A black Thunderbird bike grunted to a halt at the parking area. Rahul got down from the bike, followed by Jackal. He was still sleepy. Dressed in a windcheater, sports trousers and bandana to cover his body from the cold air, he walked towards the jogging track.

'Why the f**k did you make me get up so damn early and drag me all the way here? Rahul said in between his yawns.

'Sania informed me that Neha comes here for early morning running. She is an active member of a runners' group in Delhi and they run here frequently,' an equally sleepy Jackal replied.

'So you are planning to make me run with the girl and woo her?' Rahul's twisted face was the testimony of his surprise.

'Almost.'

'Be more specific.'

'This is the time when Neha is alone, she is all by herself. There would be no college mates ogling at you guys. You can pretend to bump into her and try and strike a conversation here.'

'Hmm... Regardless of popular opinion, I always say you are very smart Dr Jackal.'

Jackal blushed and Rahul laughed looking at him and placing his hand on his shoulders said, 'Let's find her.'

After walking around for about twenty minutes, they saw Neha in front of them. She was doing stretching exercises with a group. They were all wearing same coloured T-shirts with the name of the runners' group printed in front and the name of the runner printed on back. Rahul walked up to Neha who was wearing a halter neck tank top and black lycra leggings. The Nike head and wristband indicated her dedicated approach to the sport.

'I like the uniforms you guys are wearing,' sarcasm evident in Rahul's voice.

'Thank you for the compliment, sir,' Neha tried to hide her vexation.

'Don't call me "sir". Call me Rahul...'

'*Haa naam to suna hi hai,*' Neha cut him short with an artificial wide smile on her face. Jackal watched the ruddiness on Rahul's face listening to her reply.

'Acha listen, my friends are waiting for me, I got to go. Bye.' Neha didn't give him any chance for further dialogue and ran to join the group who had already started their running practice.

'You missed the chance,' Jackal said to Rahul in a disappointed tone.

'As if she gave me many.'

'Then go man, run behind her this is the time.' Jackal patted on Rahul's back and he hurried himself behind the group.

—⚡—

'You come here daily?' Rahul had managed to catch up with Neha.

'Yes, almost. We are a group and some of us are training for marathons too.' Neha replied while running.

'Wow, I also do cycling occasionally for fun but not much running. How about you? Ever got chance to pedal?' Rahul asked trying to control panting.

'No never.' Neha pushed herself to make sure she moved

ahead of Rahul. Rahul watched her in dismay as she took a considerable lead with ease.

'What are you doing? You are losing all the chance to become friends with her,' Jackal's sharp voice teased Rahul. He had joined him from behind.

'I am trying,' Rahul could barely speak. His lungs were winded with all the running.

'That's why I tell you charsi, quit smoking.'

'I have not come here to get health advice on smoking from you,' Rahul pushed harder and ran up to Neha.

'It's been time a long time since I practised running. I was a champion in school,' Rahul almost started following Neha.

Neha looked at him, nodded her head and put all her concentration on running. Rahul pushed even harder and reached adjacent to her. 'You run very swiftly,' words barely managed to come out from his mouth.

Neha didn't reply, but a well-built guy who was running ahead of her turned and looked at Neha's eyes checking if Rahul was stalking her.

Neha nodded her head in negation and signaled him to carry on. *I can manage him.*

She stopped and let the group carry on with running.

'You obviously didn't come here to run? Did you?' she wiped the sweat from her upper lips and forehead using the wristband.

'No...I mean yes I came here to run...with...you...' Rahul was still panting, trying hard to catch his breath.

'But you can't run Rahul Bhatia. Look at you!' Neha scorned.

'As I...said...I was...a champion in school...its just lack...of...practice...' Rahul felt challenged.

Meanwhile, Jackal had managed to join them too. Compared to Rahul he was at ease with the physical activity.

'Let's come to the point, you are stalking me Rahul,' Neha's tone was firm this time.

'Rahul wants to be friends with you,' Jackal piped in between the conversation.

Rahul was abashed. He looked at Jackal in surprise. Jackal lifted his hand. *Relax, I am making things easier for you.*

'And why should I even consider it?' Neha asked mischievously.

'Because he is a good guy...and...he is a good...runner...I mean athlete,' Jackal summed it up for her.

'Enough Jackal,' Rahul's breath was back. 'Listen Neha, I just want to be friends with you. That's all.'

'Neha Khare's friendship comes at a cost, Rahul Bhatia,' Neha looked straight into Rahul's eyes.

'What is the cost?'

'You will have to beat me in a 200-metre sprint.'

'What?'

'If you win we are friends and if you lose we go our different ways.'

Rahul sighed and looked at Jackal, who was staring at him blankly. The call to accept the challenge was going to be all his.

Rahul took a deep breath. 'Yes, I accept it. Where do we run?'

The stage was set for the 'friendship challenge run'. Two benches which were approximately 200 metres apart in a loop were identified as start and finish points. One person was stationed at the finish point to time the run. Neha's group of runners huddled behind her. She sipped some water and looked at Rahul, he was standing five metres away with Jackal on his side carrying his windcheater and bandana.

The well-built guy stood 10 metres ahead of Rahul and Neha carrying a colourful handkerchief in his hands. In a true *Fast and Furious* style, he dropped the handkerchief and both the runners sprinted.

50m in the Race

Rahul had managed to run at the same speed with Neha. He kept on turning his head towards Neha and smile at her. She on the other hand, was focused on the track ahead. The crowd behind them was cheering for their respective friends.

100m in the Race

Neha had started to lead as the distance between them increased. Her foot landing and swing of the arms were just perfect. She ran with her front foot and body slightly inclined forward, trademark of a seasoned runner. Rahul on the other hand had begun to struggle by then. His breath and his body movements were out of sync.

150m in the Race

Neha has taken a considerable lead from Rahul. She looked back over her shoulder for the first time in the race. Not finding

Rahul anywhere near her, she smiled and continued. The shouts of 'come on Neha' were far more than 'come on Rahul'.

175m in the Race

Rahul saw Neha winning the race. His heart rate was rushing faster than he was moving, his body wasn't letting him push any further. Jackal, unable to keep his excitement down ran in a reverse direction of the running loop and came adjacent to Rahul.

'RAHUL, Neha is winning. She will leave you. THIS IS YOUR ONLY CHANCE. DO IT, MAN! DO IT.' Jackal shouted.

Rahul nodded his head. The distance to go for friendship with Neha was only 25m. He gathered his will and pushed himself.

190m in the Race

Neha could sense the footsteps coming closer to her. The last 10m were the decider now. She focused on the decisive steps ahead.

195m in the Race

Neha was slightly ahead of Rahul. It was a matter of few seconds now and she was going to be the winner. *Winning is a habit for me.*

Neha was about to take the final step when she saw Rahul taking a giant leap from her behind making a war cry. His body almost flew parallel to the ground and with great force, he hit the ground before Neha's foot could land. His body skidded in the ground for some distance. Bathed in dust he lay flat on ground, head facing earth. Rahul has won the race.

Neha stopped, still in shock. Jackal jumped in exultation. Members of the runners' group were silent. They all looked at him lying down in shock and disbelief. The well-built guy was the first to clap and what followed after was resounding cheering and clapping for Rahul. They huddled around him, helped him get up and patted on his back for his crazy effort to win the race.

Neha stood aghast and looked at her friends admiring Rahul. She walked up to him and said, 'Well done, Rahul sir, I mean, Rahul. Congrats on your win.' She held her hand for handshake and Rahul held her hand. He couldn't remember the last time he was so happy.

CHAPTER 6

—∞—

This...this can't be happening. Oh God! What will I do now? I'm finished. Why did you let this happen?

M...my family will die if they find out. Noo Nooo Noooo! What should I do now...?

I...I don't have another choice. I need to stop them from knowing. Oh the shame. Oh God!

Why is this world so cruel? I have to leave...

—∞—

Rehan had been knocking on his dorm neighbour Himanshu's door now for a quarter of an hour. Rahul, Ritesh and a few other hostellers from the same floor had crowded around him.

'Are you guys sure he wasn't at dinner yesterday?' asked Rehan again, looking at his dorm-mates.

'And not even at breakfast right now?' added Ritesh.

There was a chorus of 'no', 'he might have gone out,' 'haven't seen him', 'dunno where he is', 'maybe something's wrong', from the group.

'No, he is in his room. His phone was ringing all night, Nazia just called me, she's worried because he was cutting her call over and over, and I just heard a loud thump right now, like something fell.' Rehan said anxiously.

Ritesh dialled Himanshu's cell number. Rahul put his ear to the door and confirmed it was still ringing inside. The three looked at each other and nodded. They told everyone to back up a bit and then using three powerful kicks, broke down the door.

—ᴡ—

Himanshu Mahajan was a boy from Meerut, studying Mechanical Engineering with Rehan; a straight up decent guy, very family oriented and obedient.

He was lying prone on the floor next to his bed next to two empty bottles of rum.

Rehan quickly ran in to check on Himanshu. As he turned him over, they saw he was foaming at the mouth. Rahul pointed towards three empty blister packs of Paracetamol.

Ritesh shouted, 'Call an ambulance.' He turned Himanshu over, making him face downward again and told the guys to help him open his mouth. He inserted his finger down Himanshu's throat, trying to make him puke.

—ᴡ—

Himanshu was admitted to a hospital near the college and his family was informed. The boys from the hostel waited outside the ICU; the doctor informed them that Himanshu's liver had been damaged because of the cocktail of alcohol and tablets.

'We've pumped his stomach. He needed minor surgery to reduce the swelling of his liver. We're keeping a check on him so that he doesn't become jaundiced. Have his parents been informed?' the doctor on duty asked the boys standing outside the ICU.

Rehan nodded, 'Doctor...will he be okay?'

Dr Madan looked closely at him and then the rest of the group, 'Look, this wasn't a mistake. It seems like a deliberate attempt to commit suicide. We're keeping him under observation for now. The authorities and his parents will have to deal with him, once he wakes up.'

'Can we see him?'

'He's in and out of consciousness, you can try. One person at a time, though.'

Rehan went in with trepidation. This was his class and dorm partner for over three years, lying beaten on a hospital bed. Rehan shook silently with unshed tears. He sat on the small round stool next to the bed and placed one compassionate hand on Himanshu's forehead, and holding onto his other hand. *Why did you do this my friend?*

Himanshu moved his head slightly towards Rehan's presence. His lips were dry and cracked and his skin was an abnormal waxy colour. His eyes flickered, trying to open.

'No, don't bother bhai,' Rehan said in a soft, broken tone.

Himanshu's limp fingers tightened around Rehan's, as tears dripped from his eyes; the beeping of the life support machines a stark reminder of a failed attempt. *Why did you do this?*

Rahul, Rehan and Ritesh barged out of the hospital lobby; their bloodshot eyes filled with loathing and a fire for vengeance. Between Ritesh and Rahul, they had managed to get the story out from Himanshu as to why he took such a stupid, drastic step.

All the other boys outside the hospital wing had been informed of the reason behind Himanshu's state and everyone was burning up with rage. As they crossed the lobby, the HODs of the hostellers and the engineering division, sipping cups of insipid tea, waiting for Himanshu's parents, looked at this group of exiting students with a surprised expression.

The growl of the Pulsar and Thunderbird into the south wing of the university campus, was like the sounding of a conch heralding visitors. The south wing was the den of the day scholars. Pankaj bhaiya ruled his territory from a small canteen here—be it university elections, protection of day scholars from hostellers, or selling examination question papers, all was managed from here. It was an unusual sight to see the rival gang, Rahul, Ritesh and Rehan, showing their faces in his fiefdom.

He watched as they put the bikes on their stands and walked up towards him.

'Wah wah! Brave of you to walk in here alone,' Pankaj's voice boomed around the small open enclosure. Four of his followers got up and went to stand behind his chair, facing the three newcomers.

'You must have heard about Himanshu? He tried to commit suicide today—because of you!' Ritesh spoke first, his voice barely containing the fury he felt.

Pankaj, leaning back in his chair, looked Ritesh in the eye and responded, 'What nonsense! Shheh! Anybody can gulp medicines and take my name, it does not mean I am responsible for his death or his stupidity,' Pankaj remarked coolly.

'Listen, we don't want any drama here. Just quietly come with us to the Director and acknowledge that you work as an agent of Professor Gulati and take money from students on the premise of ensuring their selection during campus placements.'

'Hahahaha...' Pankaj roared, as his cronies joined in. 'Are you seriously as dumb as you look? What the f**k are you talking about dude? Hahaha... I didn't get you.'

Rahul stepped forward menacingly and the laughter died down, 'Stop pretending, a**hole! We've verified this. Apparently, you and Gulati have a nexus—of corrupting the companies by bribing the delegates that come for campus recruitment. Gulati's tuitions, they're a front for this racket job aren't they? If you don't take extra classes with him, your name mysteriously disappears from the list of those that get to attend the interviews? You're selling seats for 10 lakhs! Himanshu had nothing. He took his father's pension and a loan against it to secure a seat, he gave it all to you and you duped him!'

'Oh look at the chikna giving a shit about others. What is it to you fag? Forget me...are you trying to blame this shit on our esteemed Professor Gulati?'

'We will not say anything, you will confess,' Rehan said quietly.

'Hahahahaha...God bless your optimism,' Pankaj laughed as he pushed his chair back roughly and walked towards the boys.

'I have been in this college for the last seven years and in the final year from the last four years. Do you think I could have managed it all alone? What if I say the HOD also gets a cut from this setting? What if I say this is all managed? Any private engineering college is only as good as the campus recruitment? With better placements comes better reputation. The more "esteemed" a college becomes, the more students queue up for admission. The longer the queue, the higher the cost of the NRI seats, higher price, better commission and business is booming. As far as recruitment is concerned, those that want it, find a way to afford it. The better the job offer, the better the pay. There are some that can afford it. That's all. It's all business—simple supply and demand fundamentals. Got it, c*****e?'

The crude logic behind his words was hard to refute. He didn't care about morality. Money, money was the key. Having this nexus confirmed right now seemed to be making the boys uncomfortable, maybe a little disappointed with their college, ashamed for the first time.

Pankaj saw the expressions on their faces and smirked, signalling one of his men to light a cigarette for him. As he took a deep drag, he continued, 'Himanshu gave me das peti to make him get a job with Styrx Ltd, the German company that was supposed to come for a campus interview next month. But the funding for their project didn't come through and they were waiting on more approvals, hence hiring got deferred. The money had been paid to everyone in the channel already and I told Himanshu to wait till the next project came in and that they would hire him. But, apparently the idiot went and attempted suicide,' Pankaj said in a wretched tone and shook his head.

He bent forward and poked Rehan's chest and said, 'You know the thing about good people is they are weak hearted, they...'

Ritesh pulled Pankaj's arm making him stumble towards him, tightened his fist and punched him hard on the face before he could finish his sentence. They heard a loud crack; Pankaj's nose had broken and he fell backwards with the shock of it. A fountain of blood oozed out from his nose. 'This is for Himanshu, g***u. This is the least you deserve.'

This unexpected move from Ritesh left everyone shocked for a second. Before Pankaj's lapdogs could make a move,

Rehan and Rahul grabbed him by his feet, dragged him out to the pavement and started landing kicks on his front and back, venting their anger, disappointment and frustration. Ritesh stood between Pankaj's four friends and them.

Rahul and Rehan grabbed the now semiconscious Pankaj and put him on their bike and drove towards the Dean's office. They knew their friend, with a black belt in Taekwondo, was more than enough for the four rookies.

Ritesh eyed the four guys, circling him cautiously. They would probably attack together. To them, four against one made better odds than taking him on one on one. Clever.

'Dum...gaand mein dum, do you have it in you?' Ritesh looked at his opponents, challenging them, goading them.

His arms took guard and he smiled, his palms inviting them to start. Years of Taekwondo practise made his sharp eyes catch the indecisive movement of the feet of the guy standing in front of him. *Hesitation?*

He jumped up straight and shot his leg out in a super-fast front kick, straight to the guy's chest. As he fell backward, clutching his ribs, Ritesh turned around. The two guys to his sides quickly held on to his arms, pulling, stretching him out, prepping him like a canvas for the third guy to hit him. Ritesh used them as a support to use both his legs and kick the third guy. He too fell backwards, stumbling over the plastic table and chairs and getting lost in the rubble. *This is my favourite move.*

It was Ritesh who was now holding on to the guys on his left and right. As he jumped backwards, he used the momentum and his upper body core strength to pull them together and make them smash against each other. The one on the right stumbled and fell, while the one on his left jumped towards him. Ritesh swiftly managed a pivot on his right leg, and with his left, landed a harsh kick to the guy's jaw. He fell to the ground, out for the count.

The guy on his right hand straightened up and ran towards Ritesh, his fist pulled back. Ritesh side stepped his attack and held on to the guy's fist. He twisted his arm around to his back and shoved him forward an arm's length. Raising his leg, and letting go of the guy's arm, he kicked hard. He went straight into the concrete pillar and slid down unconscious. *Two men down two more to go.*

He looked at the guy still trying to get up under the mess of plastic furniture. *They are losing it.*

He turned around to see what happened to the first guy. He was lying on the edge of the canteen, holding onto his chest, breathing heavily but with eyes closed. *Did he hit his head or is he pretending?*

The sound of the clatter of chairs being pushed aside made Ritesh turn around.

The guy was wheezing, hunched and holding onto his ribcage. He saw his three friends out for the count and stepped backwards hurriedly, '*Mada***od! Tu ruk!* Stay here, I am calling my friends they will teach you a lesson.'

Ritesh saw him running away. A faint smile crossed his face. He walked towards his Pulsar and drove towards the Dean's office.

—⁓—

'Do you know what nonsense are you talking?' Director Rajeshwar Agrawal shook his head as he stood from his chair.

The heroics of Rahul, Ritesh and Rehan had reached the ears of every student in the university before sundown. The hostllers versus day scholars rivalry reached a new pinnacle.

The hostller gang leaders had shown the audacity to barge into the day scholars den and kidnap their leader to be presented at the director's office. The very same morning a hosteller had attempted suicide. This news had become university headline. Both the supporters and opponents of the engineering division were rallying outside the administrative offices, shouting for the director to take action. And now these three, his favourite, outstanding guys were telling him about corruption in his offices. *Something big was cooking.*

'Yes, sir, we're not lying. This nexus exists in our engineering division. You can make an investigation committee and probe. Pankaj Bhoj will testify,' Rehan said.

'I am not going to tell a lie, these guys came to canteen and beat me, sir.' Pankaj blabbered. His broken nose testifying his words. 'Himanshu didn't attempt suicide because of any money paid to any campus recruitment nexus. He did it because his girlfriend Nazia Ali was getting married to someone else as soon as the final term of the college gets over. Nazia is from an orthodox family, sir. They did not like her affair with Himanshu. They want her to get married to a Muslim. You can check their phone records. Ask mutual friends. They are a couple. This is why he wanted to die.'

'Lies!! This isn't true. Himanshu will testify before the comm...' Rahul started, in Himanshu's defence. Rehan placed his hand on Rahul's shoulder to stop him.

'Sir, whatever is the issue between Himanshu and Nazia and their families, that's a different thing. It has nothing to do with why he took this drastic step. He will confirm it to you. We leave this matter to you and the investigation committee.'

After a couple of minutes, the director was still looking out of his office window at the crowd outside, 'May we leave now, sir?' Rehan enquired.

'It's not as easy as you think, you troublemakers,' Professor Sudeep Gulati entered the room and with him the SHO of Faridabad Police Station, leaving all those in the room stunned.

Rahul turned towards the director and said, 'Sir, this is not fair, we have not done anything.'

'What is the meaning of this, professor?' questioned the director.

Professor Gulati in his slimy tone asserted, 'Sir, these boys can't beat fellow students and threaten to kill them. All four friends of Pankaj have lodged a police complaint against these three. You should rusticate them. It's time for them to pack their bags.'

Ritesh, Rahul, and Rehan looked at Director Agarwal. He was furious that this matter was taken outside the university, 'Is this necessary SHO sahib?' he addressed the police officer.

'Sir, they'll have to come with us to the station.'

Pankaj Bhoj and Professor Sudeep Gulati's gleeful expressions said it all.

CHAPTER 7

—~~~—

They looked like revolutionaries; the three young men being escorted out by the police, hordes of students lined up outside. They looked at myriad faces—on one side, those that looked proud, shaken, curious, worried, fearful and sympathetic; and the other, grinning, sneering, contemptuous, and ecstatic over this turn of affairs. This moment scrolled passed slowly for them. Rehan noticed Nazia's teary, grateful face; to Rahul what stood out was Neha's startled confusion. Ritesh nodded towards an anxious Jackal, trying to offer comfort even as they were shuffled into the police van, to the chants of 'we're with you, free the innocent.'

Professor Gulati, standing on steps at the entrance of the block, looked over the commotion, a malicious smile on his face. He took the rimless glasses off his slender nose and wiped them with his handkerchief. *Huh, these dust particles are easy wipes.*

As he put his spectacles back on, he turned around and walked back into the building, leaving his colleagues to marshal the crowd back to their classes. The students slowly dissipated; the chanting dying down into broken whispered conversations.

—~~~—

They sat facing each other in a close circle inside the police lockup, the only occupants of this 6x8 foot room. Ritesh looking very disturbed asked, 'Guys, did you ever stop to wonder what the problem is with people today? The system is so screwed up. Whatever we did, we did for the good of someone, we did it for justice, and we did it because it was the right thing to do; to punish a wrongdoer. Crooks like Bhoj and Gulati are thriving, roaming around freely without any consequences and us...? We're the one's having to deal with situations like these. Those who raise their voice against a problem are the ones that get persecuted. I'd read somewhere, when exposing a crime is treated as committing a crime, you're ruled by criminals!'

Ritesh's anger erupted in the form of frustrated anguish. His friends had nothing to offer to calm him down. He looked at the room adjacent to theirs, the shoddily dressed policemen, one chewing what smelled like gutka, another talking to a man who was requesting him to file an FIR for over 30 minutes.

'You know what's required? People like us, kids, and youngsters to take the lead. We all need some serious dum! *G mein dum!* You know what I mean? We are the future of this country and we should stop taking things for granted. We need GMD in our generation. Losers cannot make a winning nation, we can't let others make decisions for us or let them define us. We need to be able to control our own destiny. Each for his own united for a common goal. That's all! You know what? We're in jail right now because we took a stand and refused to let a wrong thing continue...I'd do it again. Anytime!' his rage against the establishment and the unfairness of it expended, leading to a deafening silence.

The three boys spent the next hour turning over Ritesh's words in their heads and remembering the past eight hours.

The banging of the wooden laathi against the iron bars of their lockup made them look up. The sub inspector on duty was resting on the desk closest to their room.

'SHO saab did not file the FIR against you people. He knows if he does that your career will be finished. No company would hire you if there is a police case against you. We are calling your parents and asking them to submit a written apology to the college and sign a bond as insurance, to police that you people would not create any ruckus in future.'

He looked at the three boys with scorn, 'Get real in life boys, you won't reach anywhere if you continue to do this useless stuff in college.'

Ritesh, Rahul and Rehan all looked at him with visible loathing as he walked back to his station.

After a pause Ritesh said, 'My parents are in Punjab, they'll take time to reach.'

'Ammi and abba will also take time to reach. Can you call your dad, Rahul? Delhi isn't far. Would he come and take our guarantee?' Rehan asked.

'I don't care whether they inform him or not or what he does. Best not to depend on him,' said Rahul bitterly. Ritesh and Rehan weren't surprised. Rahul had never been comfortable discussing his parents. Although he was from Delhi, a mere two-hour-drive away, he still chose to stay in the hostel away from home.

'Are you sure?' asked Rehan softly.

Rahul looked to the side, avoiding the question.

Ritesh placed a hand over Rahul's shoulder, 'Are you okay, bro? I think it's time...'

Rahul shrugged, contemplating whether to finally share

or not. He had never shared exactly why he wasn't fond of his family. He spoke after a pause, 'My father killed my mom.'

Ritesh and Rehan exchanged stunned looks.

'What?'

'Why?'

'Rajesh Bhatia was and is a workaholic. He has always been like this ever since I remember. His real marriage was to his work and company. My mother never got his attention, love or time. He was always travelling, always busy with meetings and accumulating wealth. He completely forgot that there was a kid and a wife always waiting for him at home. Mom lived like she was a widow. I remember fights, her tears, and her excuses when he didn't turn up for birthdays or anniversaries or occasions. She tried being both my mother and father, but...' Rahul narrated his story in a monotone.

'Loneliness began to eat my mom and she got herself involved in kitty parties and began finding solace in alcohol. Alcohol is funny; it's the solution and cause of all of life's problems. My happy-go-lucky mom, full of life was drinking her sorrows away. The more she depended on it, the faster it began to drain her and take her away from us. She had a stroke one day. A big one. Her already frail and wilting body couldn't take the strain. Her psychiatrist was there too, when I reached the hospital. I overheard them talking, she died of a broken heart. In her last moments too, while I held her cold hands, her eyes searched for my father...but Mr Rajesh Bhatia was in Mumbai, closing a multi-million dollar deal.'

'I hate my father for what he did to my mom. He killed her, he took her life, took her away from me, made me an orphan,' Rahul broke down, after letting his pent up anguish out. Saying it out loud made it all the more real and for the first time he had been able to speak to someone about it.

Rehan leant to his side and hugged Rahul, as his body shook with silent sobs. Ritesh closed his eyes, finally understanding the cause for his friends' pain; he gripped Rahul's knee in support.

They were lying down, quietly staring at the lock up ceiling when a few hours later a constable unlocked the iron frame door. He signalled them to get up, 'Time to go boys.'

They exchanged a quick glance between them as they got up. *Hostel Warden would have come to rescue us...*

They stepped out and saw a man sitting with the SHO, laughing at a shared joke. His black coat and mannerisms indicated he might be a lawyer. They stumbled forward in surprise when the officer in charge noticed them. He sobered up and preached, 'This is no time to do ruckus in college. You all belong to good families, spend your time in studies, score good marks and get a good job. Am I clear?'

'Next time if I find you guys repeating this sort of mistake I will straightaway file an FIR. Got it?'

The three boys nodded at the issued instructions.

'Rajput sahib, you can take them now.'

At this the man in the black coat stood up, shook the SHO's hands with gratitude and signalled to the boys to follow him.

The boys followed this man out, exchanging a curious expression amongst themselves. *Who is this?*

On exiting the station, they saw a BMW sedan parked outside. Mr Bhatia Senior had come, after all. With his head down, Rahul walked quietly towards the car. The window rolled down halfway and Rajesh Bhatia's two spoken words were brittle enough to shatter glass, 'Get in.' Rahul turned to wave good bye to his friends and saw that they were being shepherded by the lawyer into his car. They looked back with concerned expressions and disappeared inside the car.

The journey back home to their home at Jor Bagh from the Faridabad police station was quiet. Rajesh was busy working on his laptop, choosing to not to speak in front of the chauffeur. Rahul stared out the car window the entire two and a half hour journey. As soon as the car stopped in the driveway of their bungalow, Rahul got out in a hurry and slammed the car door shut. Rahul was hurrying towards his room on the first floor when his father held him back, 'Do you know what would have happened had I not reached on time?' Rahul stopped but didn't turn.

'"Steel baron's son caught in a college brawl!" would have been the headlines tomorrow. You obviously don't care about the family image or business reputation. The director of your university knows me personally and he informed me about your "heroics". I immediately called up the Faridabad Police station and paid the SHO to refuse to write a FIR against you boys. If I would not have acted in time you and your friends' careers would have been finished by now.' Mr Rajesh Bhatia's small frame shook with anger while speaking.

Rahul kept quiet.

'Why do you have to get into such brawls? I have sent you there to study, just do that and join the business.'

'Dad, they run a nexus in the college. They take money...'

'I don't care what they do,' He was cut short by an angry wave by his father. 'This is how the world is. Cruel and opportunist. You can't change it. You can't fight for all. Nobody fought for your grandfather when he came penniless from Lahore. He fought his own battle and created this empire. Don't waste your energy in such petty things. You have to take this empire further from here. I want you to become an emperor.'

'I don't want all this,' Rahul finally looked straight at his father, his defiance firm and obvious. 'I want to be free, from you, from your reticent world. You want me to become a cold-blooded monster like you, who killed my mom.'

That his dad was furious was evident, but that he would step forward and slap him hard was unexpected.

Rahul stumbled back from the shock, as Rakesh baba, their loyal man-Friday, rushed to support him.

―᚜―

As Rehan and Ritesh walked into their canteen, they heard an odd assortment of broken voices amidst an unnatural silence, like they entered a vacuum. The TV set was on, relaying some breaking news, but it was the kids' expressions that surprised them. There were people sitting huddled up, comforting each other, a bunch of girls crying and being consoled by those surrounding them; groups of guys discussing something ardently; people scattered around the canteen and also waiting for the payphone at the counter. All of them, staring in one direction, towards the television.

Rehan and Ritesh rushed forward towards Jackal, nearest to the television set his four crooked fingers at his lips, his nervousness apparent.

'What's happened?' enquired both the boys together, wondering if their arrest had made the news. He looked at them all shaken up, and pointed towards the TV.

The news anchor, also visibly upset was stringing together broken sentences trying to make sense of the happenings. The ticker at the bottom of the screen flashed the headlines: 'BOMB BLASTS IN CAPITAL CITY', 'DELHI HIT BY A SERIES OF BOMB BLASTS'.

Someone turned up the volume, the news correspondent standing in what seemed like a crowded market place announced he was at the site of the first blast at Sarojini Nagar Market and that this blast was followed by two more at Paharganj and Greater Kailash in quick succession. The casualties were as yet unknown, but the count of the injured was pegged to be at 70 in total already. They were calling it a planned terrorist attack cutting through the pulse of a vibrant nation at its very heart.

Ritesh could feel the blood pounding in his ears, his feet cemented to the floor. Many of his cousins, college friends and their families were from New Delhi. The images that were being telecast were heart wrenching. The helplessness of those around him matched the agony of the crowd seen on the television screen. Watching and absorbing this inadequate emptiness made him restless. He wanted to help these people, to do something for them, help them get past this tragedy; but more than that he wanted to avenge those that had suffered. This moment felt like a spark of something to Ritesh. A small ember lit up within him.

A Few Months Later

The northern end of the Aravalli range of mountains consisted of isolated hills and scattered rocky ridges in parts of Haryana and south Delhi. The lost lake of Mangar forest, a beautiful small water body adjacent to the Mahadev temple, was a sacred area for the locals. The trails in this forest were ideal for mountain bikers, calling out to the cycling enthusiasts.

Rahul, Rehan and Ritesh had stumbled onto this generally uninhabited jewel in the hustle and bustle of the national capital region. The quiet trails were ideal for mountain bikers. The three friends had found a common passion of cycling and had built on it to become semi-pro bikers. Their cycling gear; helmets, sunglasses and gloves were lying next to them as they rested on boulders overlooking the lake atop a small hill; their bikes leaning against the majestic gulmohar tree nearby. It was on this hilltop that they had befriended an old man, whom they referred to as Mangar Baba. He offered them advice with a cup of tea every time they made their way up his hill.

'Guys, we're nearly done with college...do you realize? Shit. Where did the time go...? The seventh semester exams are right around the corner, we need to prepare for them,' Rahul broke the silence.

'More importantly, we need to figure out what we want to achieve in life,' Rehan added emphatically.

They both looked at Ritesh, who was staring at the lake silently, his mood contemplative.

'I want to contribute to society,' Ritesh said after a pause.

'You want to become a social worker?' Rahul asked with mock shock.

'Not really... You can contribute to the nation and society in other ways also,' Ritesh answered.

'I just want to contribute to the real estate of the country,' Rehan said with a wink. First, take a high-paying MNC job out of the country. I will take ammi and abbu with me. And second, when I have a million dollars in my bank I'll come back to India, invest in real estate and cool my heels off for the rest of my life. That's it!' Rehan smirked as he put his hand behind his head and lay back on the rock.

Rahul shook his head slightly, amused by Rehan's naive enthusiasm, wishing he too could share it. He lit a cigarette he was playing with, took a deep drag and said, 'I...want to run away from my family. Run away from this place, maybe even this country. I don't know what I want to become. I'll take just any goddamn job and leave.'

Ritesh looked towards Rahul. His hand whipped up and snatched the burning cigarette out from his friend's mouth and stubbed it out on the rock.

'You have got to drop this damn thing! It'll kill you before I die!' Ritesh reiterated his one point of dissension with Rahul. Rahul rolled his eyes at him.

'Look, my mom and dad always believed in doing what they wanted to, what their heart told them is right, whether or not what society deemed fit. You've met them; you know what they're like. They hate imposing their views on anyone. Dad converted my dadaji's bungalow into an old age home and runs a school for differently abled kids. Mum's also following her passion of painting. She loves being an artist and teaching photography and fine arts to the students. They live in a section of the old house with the other residents and take care of them. They're highly content in life.'

'They let me figure out my own stream for college, and are giving me a chance to figure out what I want to do next; get a job with an MNC, do my MBA, or whatever. I spoke to them a few days ago, and they had said the same thing even then that

I need to figure out what's my calling in life. What my heart wants to do—irrespective of any duties and responsibilities as the only son. They said, "Choose that what excites you—something you'd want to wake up for everyday and lose your sleep for. Only then will all your effort be worth it."'

'So what *excites* you my friend?' Rahul raised his eyebrows mischievously.

'I don't know what "excites" me yet, but I feel agitated when I see helpless people; you know, like when someone's suffering, or when the weak are bullied; when someone loses their sense of security, it makes me edgy. If only people stood up for one another and supported—instead of bringing each other down; where brotherhood would be more than a word, but a way of life. Society has lost its way; the way we disrespect humanity, society, people and cultures; the way the world today disrespects elders, women and even men; the way businesses are run, with bribes and money; the way we've lost our ethics in the struggle to be powerful; the way our relationships are intertwined with ego and blackmail. We're all weak-willed cowards,' Ritesh ended his monologue with his hands fisted together and barely contained resentment.

'So why don't you join politics? The nation wants and needs young energetic leaders like you,' Rehan said, laying a calming hand on Ritesh's arm.

'This is the core issue, Rehan; we all want someone else to do it. *You become leader and do it for me.* There seems to be an attitude problem, as if we cannot shake ourselves out of the mindset of limited achievement.Why can't there be a leader in all of us? All of us can take the responsibility to contribute in some form or the other to give something back to the society, back to the nation. We become doctors, engineers, businessmen for nothing but selfish reasons today, earning and living for ourselves and our family. What happened to the greater good? We should all contribute something. What happened to being responsible and doing something for your country? It can start from as small as not throwing litter on the roads. Giving back is the ultimate stage reached by the enlightened men and women.' Ritesh responded.

'Dude, I think you are confused between nationality and spirituality. Both of them can't exist simultaneously,' countered Rahul.

'Rahul, that's the catch. Being spiritual will make your thoughts more holistic and vice versa,' replied Ritesh.

Amid the pause for breath between Rahul and Ritesh, Rehan intervened, 'Relax guys, this isn't a debate show on TV where "India wants to know". He mocked a famous TV anchor. He continued, 'There'll always be time for arguing, but right now in case you've noticed the sunlight's fading; we need to get back.'

The three boys looked out towards the horizon, the lengthening shadows giving them a push to get up and going. Rahul tackled Ritesh in a mock fight, easing the seriousness of the moment as Rehan donned his cycling gear. Rahul had gifted them a matching set of gloves, helmets and wind sheeters to truly make them a team, in everything they did. As they wore their helmet and gloves Ritesh said, 'One day you'll leave this world behind...so live a life you will remember'. Rahul shook his head with amusement and Ritesh returned Rehan's smile with his own.

The large frame of Scott Scale 80 mountain bike landed on the dusty trail hidden between small rocks. The Aravalli mountain trail on the Gurgaon-Faridabad border can be dangerous for riders if they are not careful. Rahul's strong arm grabbed the handle steadily and guided the bike downhill. It was getting dark and the trio rode back on the twisty trail to the university. They rode one after the other like three musketeers. They pedalled hard, ditching the bushes with sharp thorns and jumped few rocks to reach the university campus, bathed in sweat and filled with positive energy.

The day scholars hadn't forgotten about their mortifying defeat at the hands of the hostellers a few weeks ago. Bhoj's faction had assumed that Rahul, Rehan and Ritesh would be shunned by everyone for having gone to jail, but instead they returned as heroes. The animosity between the two groups was at a peak. Small scuffles broke out among them every day, all under the radar of the college administration.

The hostellers had strict orders from their three leaders, not to start any fights; defense, when required, but no offensive measures should be taken. Pankaj Bhoj's loyalists on the other hand had decided to teach the three mavericks a lesson; they had after all walked into their boss's den, given him a beating and literally dragged bhaiya ji across the university campus. This was now a matter of collective pride.

A group of Pankaj's friends from another top private university based out of Noida were on a visit to the MSU campus. Ardent supporters of bhaiya ji, whose reputation was unavoidable in the university circuits, this group had come to offer their respects to him before the upcoming exams; mostly in the hopes that he would have copies of their upcoming question papers. They offered their services to win back bhaiya ji's reputation in the college. Along with the MSU seniors, these five outsiders hatched a plan.

―⚬―

Dusk had just about fallen on the campus, when five boys entered the C wing of the MSU hostel. One of the day scholar juniors had overheard Rehan, Ritesh and Rahul making plans for later that day during breakfast in the main canteen. While Rehan would be staying back in his room all day and studying, Ritesh and Rahul would go on their habitual bi-weekly bike ride.

Rehan, they knew by reputation, was not a gunda. More decent than the other two, he was going to be an easy catch.

The boys carried with them nothing but a folded up blanket.

―⚬―

The hostel wing was nearly deserted at this hour, with most of the seniors on the floor having gone to tea. The boys quickly walked the length of the corridor, stopping at a door they were told led to Rehan's room.

They tried the door handle and a voice from inside asked who it was. The boys quickly shuffled in and shut the lights. By the faint tungsten glow from the room's only window, they overpowered Rehan. They threw the blanket over him, pushed him to the floor and landed punches and kicks; all five together. The moans and screams emitting from under the blanket let them know that their 'kambal kutai' was a success. This treatment was usually reserved for ragging nights and fights in the boys' hostel, some even made it a tradition on birthdays, although the kicks and punches given then were lighter and more in jest. Today, it was a beating, aimed to hurt, to avenge bhaiya ji's hurt reputation. How dare these hostellers beat Pankaj Bhoj! The boys stopped kicking when they were exhausted. Breathing heavily and exhausted, they finally let up. As one of them bent down to check if Rehan was still breathing, he said, 'This is Pankaj Bhaiya's answer to you. Next time, don't even dare to look at him in the eye!' He pulled the blanket off Rehan's face.

All five of the Noida boys jumped back in shock, two of them tripped and fell. They had been shown Rehan's photo on someone's cell phone earlier, but this...this couldn't be him. Even with the swollen and bleeding face, no one would say this was Rehan. This guy was a monster.

Jackal's bald head, caked with blood and bruises was swelling up in places. He turned his face around and stared at the five boys, one of his amber eyes swollen shut. He raised his four-fingered hand up in front of them, looking past the misshapen angles, he croaked, 'They won't leave you. You better run...'

The assaulters looked at each other and realized they beat up the wrong guy. *Shit.*

They ran.

'*Khoon ka badla khoon,*' said one hosteller.

'Shut up, no melodrama here,' said Ritesh. He was furious. He placed his palm on Jackal's head. He had been treated, bandaged up and was sleeping now, thanks to some really strong painkillers. Thankfully nothing was broken, but his friend had received a lot of bruises. Jackal would be sore for a while.

'Are you sure you guys didn't recognize them?' Rahul asked again, looking at the third years that found Jackal like this. They had seen a bunch of guys running down the stairs in a rush as they were coming up. Rohit and his friend had then run towards the rooms to see what was wrong, and they found Jackal passed out with the door open.

Rohit shook his head, 'They weren't from our college. For sure.'

Jackal had briefly come to senses when Rahul, Ritesh and Rehan had arrived. He told them that this was arranged by Pankaj, 'They kept saying bhaiya ji's revenge.'

'Why Jackal, though? Do you think they got confused and were actually after Rehan? His room is next door...' Rahul mused out loud.

Ritesh cut in, 'It doesn't matter. Rehan or Jackal, or anyone else—we're all the same. If he attacks anyone of us, we all bleed. We're one,' he said looking around the room. 'This will never end. Blood for blood and bones for bones! If we have to hit Pankaj, we have to finish him once and for all,' Ritesh looked at Rehan and Rahul.

Rehan looked up from his hands and said, 'I think it's time for "Gulu gulu...".'

Rahul smiled and started dialling a number from his mobile.

Present Day, Delhi Airport

10 October 2011, 11.30 p.m.

Rahul placed his iPhone to his ears.

'Yeah, Rahul?'

'Rehan, I just landed at the Delhi airport. I'll be taking a cab to AIIMS. Where are you now?'

'I've also reached Delhi railway station and heading towards the taxi stand. I should reach AIIMS in 30 to 40 minutes,' Rehan replied.

'Okay. See you at the hospital,' Rahul cut the line.

He boarded a cab and threw in his hand bag, 'Bhaiya, AIIMS, as fast as you can.'

As the driver accelerated away from the airport, he increased the volume of the radio, Rahul heard the presenter announce the next song, 'Laila O Laila' from the hit Bollywood film *Qurbani*.

A slow smile spread across his face as the song began to play.

CHAPTER 8

Third Floor, Boys Hostel
Six Years Ago, 2005

Gulu gulu...gulu gulu...hey hey hey...bubub...bubub...hey hey...!

Sultry actress Zeenat Aman gyrated to the thumping beats of a wigged Amjad Khan drumming on the screen. The boys had sourced a CD of the movie *Qurbani*, the song, 'Laila O Laila' being playing on loop in Rahul's laptop. The core team of planners were sitting in Jackal's room hashing out their strategy.

'Okay, we need to be clever about this. One stone, two birds. Hear me out. So, we know Professor Gulati aka Gullu,' started off Ritesh, 'has been running his operation for a few years now. He used to do the same old thing, pressurize students, our seniors to attend his own tuition. If they attended someone else's tuition classes, he would fail them during vivas, give them lower marks, misplace their papers and the like; get them in trouble by calling their parents and tattling on them till such time they succumbed to his pressure. A lot of students gave in to his tactics, but a bunch of them actually got very tired of this. Like us, these seniors—the crazy, naughty, brilliant minds got together one night and hatched a plan. They wanted to give Gulati a taste of his own medicine.'

A few third years were listening to this story for the first time. They looked at and heard Ritesh with rapt attention.

He continued, 'Amjad Khan singing "Gulu gulu..." really hit the right chord with them. It was like it was meant to be. They started with harmless phone calls. Cells were fairly rare and new in the campus. Some rich kids got a hold of a few and started making calls to Gulati. He used to feel mighty proud he owned a cell phone when no other faculty did. Of course he could afford it; minting money from students for his scams. Every time he answered, they played this song. They said nothing, no other voice or noise; just the song.

Rehan piped up, 'They'd be calling him every 10 minutes or so; on his office line, his mobile, his residence line; everywhere. The calls happened all day and night for weeks. Then he started ignoring the calls. Let it keep ringing. Didn't answer any calls at all, not even genuine ones apparently. Then, he started threatening after picking up—yelling and abusing. He, of course, didn't know who was behind it.

'He couldn't work, couldn't eat, and couldn't screw up things peacefully. He started getting irritated. He would yell at all the kids in class the next morning but couldn't take any action as he had no proof of who it was. Nonetheless, the calls didn't stop. He finally gave up and decided that he'll not take lectures for the rest of the semester. Another professor was appointed and the kids breathed a sigh of relief,' Rahul concluded.

'Where does this take us?' Dr Jackal asked.

'Two points, first, Gulati hates being called "Gullu", especially this song, we will irritate him to the core, and second, we will use the sweet candy to lull him into our trap, greedy bastard that he is. He'll come running. With him being occupied with irritation and lechery we will play with his mind. He will break open. Bhoj's strength too gets taken away. We'll get rid of both of them once and for all. I want to end this corporate nexus! No bones broken, no blood sprinkled,' Ritesh concluded.

'Also, the hostellers, in one shot will sit on the throne of supremacy,' Rahul added.

'But what will be this "sweet candy" that will tempt Gulati?' asked Jackal.

'Now that we are taking lessons from history, our mythology also tells us that for every Vishwamitra there is a Menaka,' Rehan jumped up from the table he was sitting on.

'I know of one Menaka!' Rahul said with a grin.

He found Neha in the canteen. So much had happened since they had last spoken. Between Himanshu's suicide attempt and their stint in jail, his regular family shit and tiff with dad, and now Jackal's beating, Neha had only been at the back of his mind, a solace, a place to hide when things got too much. He'd been catching glimpses of her, exchanging nothing but soft glances with her on and off.

She was as always impeccably dressed; casual chic in her fitted denims and T-shirt, and shades on her head. He walked over to her table, full of giggling girls and a few boys, and half-eaten food.

'Neha,' Rahul called out as he reached her. With his hands in his jeans pockets, wearing a loose sweatshirt and perfectly messed up gelled hair; he knew why the girls around him were staring. He was used to it. But he had eyes only for this one girl.

Neha turned to look at him, 'Hi, Rahul, uh...sir.'

Rahul smiled down at her, 'Just Rahul is fine. I need to...'

'Did you have a good time in the police lock-up?' piped up the guy sitting next to Neha, in a mocking tone.

Rahul looked daggers at him, but what surprised him was Neha's reaction.

'Don't be such an a**hole, Sumit.'

Rahul looked at her curiously. The entire table had quietened down and was staring at them. Their eyes playing ping pong, looking left to right between him and Neha.

'Sumit, is it? You're lucky I don't deal with garbage,' Rahul said with a smile.

He felt Neha's hand on his arm, as she tried to guide him away from the table.

Rahul looked at Sumit whose eyes were glued to Neha's hand on his arm. He understood.

Neha turned to look at him, 'Are we going or not?'

Rahul promptly stepped to the side, bent down and whispered, 'After you, my lady.'

'My friends are crazy about you, you know?' Neha volunteered as they took a walk around the central park in front of the canteen. 'Well, the girls in any case.'

Rahul laughed softly, 'If you say so. I didn't notice.'

Neha looked up at him, a slight blush stealing into her cheeks.

'I know why the boys hate me,' he looked down at her pointedly.

She shook her head and laughed it off.

'So, how have you been? Did they keep you in the lock up for a long time?'

'No... I was out the same day, went home after, so you might have missed seeing me here.'

'Oh okay. Good. You stay in Delhi?'

'Yep.'

They were almost at a quiet corner of the lawn when Rahul asked, 'Do you want to sit? I need to discuss something very important with you.'

She sat and looked up at him with a quiet expectant smile on her face.

He turned his face up to the sky. *God! She's beautiful.*

'Look, I need to explain some things first, so hear me out,' Rahul started. He explained to her the history of antagonism between the day scholars and hostellers, the circumstances under which Himanshu took the extreme step of suicide and the resultant fight between his gang and Pankaj Bhoj.

Rahul was very carefully gauging Neha's expressions, to figure out whether she understood. He paused for breath as he discussed the stint in the police station and the conversation they had with Ritesh.

She held up her hand to stop him, 'You know Rahul... I really felt for you guys when they took you in. It was very unfair,' she said softly. 'You didn't return with the others for a few days and I was worried about you, because well, you're like this heroic Bollywood gunda? I thought you might have beaten up a cop or something,' she ended on a slightly mischievous note.

Rahul started laughing.

'But I'm very pleased you did what you guys did. Pankaj Bhoj needs a kick up the ass.'

'Neha, I'm glad you said that...because, we...ah...need your help. We have a plan that will take down Gulati and Bhoj together and we were hoping you'd help us.'

He quickly ran through the plan with Neha and her role in it.

Neha heard him out and wondered whether it would work. She asked Rahul, 'Why me?'

'Well, firstly, we needed a new face. You're still relatively new. With any other senior girl, he'll trace it back to us. Secondly, we needed someone that looks like an angel but can deal with idiots like him, if required. Nobody better than you for that I think.' Rahul grinned.

'And third...?'

'Thirdly and lastly, I choose you.'

She blushed.

He held out his hand, 'Are you in? Would you help us out? Help me out?'

Neha placed her hand in his and nodded, 'Yes.'

The pure joy on Rahul's face stunned her for a second. The sun's last rays were shining on his face, making his eyes glint. *Oh...he's gorgeous. I might be falling for him.*

Rahul looked at Neha's hand resting comfortably in his. They held on for a little longer.

—☸—

'Gulati sir.'

Neha, dressed in her sexiest halter top and tight skirt, walked into Professor Gulati's cabin. Her eyes lined with deep dark kohl and full lips brushed with a red tint matched her sexy voice.

'I want to join your Brilliant Tuition classes.'

Professor Gulati was working on some papers at his desk. The cabin lights were dimmed, only a table lamp was on. He didn't even look up at her as he said in a monotone, 'You'll have to take an entrance test.' The 'Brilliant Tuition' classes were his infamous entrepreneurial venture.

'But sir,' Neha's voice took on a whinny tone as she walked forward to the edge of Gulati's table; her heels tapping on the wooden flooring.

He looked up as she bent low over his desk, resting her elbows on the table top, flashing him her cleavage.

'I'm from this college itself. You can take me...just like that,' she snapped her fingers.

Gulati stared at her, expressionless, 'Rules are rules. There will be a notification of the entrance test. You may leave.'

He buried his head back in his papers, totally unaffected by her.

—∞—

'Are you sure he's into girls? He didn't even letch.' Neha walked into Rahul's room ten minutes later.

All the boys inside gaped at her.

She turned to look at them once she shut the room door again, laughing. 'Oh, come on! Well, this is exactly what I'm talking about. You guys just had the normal reaction to a girl walking in wearing her sexiest outfit.'

Rahul stood up and went to Neha. 'You want a jacket or something? It's cold outside.'

'Okay.'

As she took Rahul's leather jacket from him, she looked at Ritesh and said, 'Zilch. He was like stone. This didn't work.'

'That's strange, as per our calculations and his general outlook of life he should be a straight up restless tharki,' Rahul looked at Rehan who was equally clueless.

The core team looked at each other in dismay, trying to figure it out. Their ace stroke of making Gulati desire something and then taking it away from him had just fallen flat.

'Do you think he's the sati-savitri kind?' Rehan thought out loud, to the horrified looks of his companions.

'Haha. What a joke. No! He may be treading cautiously though... He may have changed over a period of time. He knows all eyes are on him and he will not get sucked in so easily,' Ritesh mulled.

An uneasy silence followed Ritesh's words, when there was a cough from the bed.

'Guys, I think what Rahul said was the key,' said Jackal, sitting up straighter, well on his way to recovery. Only a few black and blue marks were visible under his shirt and a few cuts on his face. He kept his rounded ribcage bandaged and ate a good number of painkillers in a day to walk around. Today was his first day out of his own room.

'Jackal, what do you mean?' asked Rahul surprised.

'We're expecting him to be a straight up restless tharki...' said Jackal with a devilish grin. 'I think I can crack him.'

The team stared at Jackal for a few seconds before they got it. Neha slapped her hand to her mouth and burst out laughing.

Ritesh, Rahul and Rehan looked at each other and then Jackal with surprised expressions. Jackal had usually only contributed to the planning, never the action. They looked at him with renewed hope and pride. The room had a sudden resurgence of mischievousness.

Professor Gulati was marching down the corridor a few days later. The thinning white hair on his head indicated roughly the five decades he had spent in this world. He seemed preoccupied.

Perfect.

His eyes were on the papers in his hands, not looking where he was going.

'Ouch.'

'Be careful, young man,' said Gulati looking up at Jackal as all his papers fell to the floor.

'Oh... Huh... I'm so sorry, sir,' Jackal bent delicately to help Gulati with his papers.

Gulati bent down as well, at eye level with Jackal who was glancing at him on and off, shyly.

'It's okay. Thank you. Be careful next time, boy,' Gulati said softly as he stared at Jackal's abnormalities.

Jackal nodded, got up and walked away slowly.

He had only walked down a couple of steps away when Gulati called out to him, 'Young man...'

Breathing a sigh of relief, Jackal turned shyly.

'Yes, sir,' he said in a soft voice.

'Are you alright, you look a little...ill,' enquired Gulati.

'I am not ill, sir, I am ill fated,' replied Jackal.

'I didn't quite understand?'

'It's a long story sir, leave it, it will be of no interest to you,' Jackal replied dejectedly and turned around to walk away. His mannerism hooked Gulati's attention.

'Wait,' he said in a slimy, caring tone, holding on to Jackal's arm. 'I have time and I think I can help you. Meet me at 8.00 p.m., tonight after I finish the tuition classes and we will talk.'

Jackal watched Gulati disappearing into a classroom at the end of the corridor. He looked out towards the grounds, and spotted his friends and Neha standing near the bike stand. They were looking in his direction. He signalled a 'thumbs up' to them.

Neha looking towards the corridor imagined Gulati and Jackal holding hands and running in slow motion around the pillars, with music in the background straight out of an '80's Bollywood flick. She shook her head to share her wild thoughts with the boys and turned to see them enveloped in boy hugs. She started laughing at the kiddish behavior these supposedly three macho men were displaying. Rahul turned around and enveloped her in a bear hug, taking her by surprise. The whistles from Ritesh and Rehan were enough to have them jump away from each other, their faces red.

CHAPTER 9

—⚌—

Jackal was waiting patiently in a dark corner of the corridor, watching the students file out of the classroom Gulati used for his Brilliant Tuition classes. He was equipped with the spy pen recorder that Ritesh had sourced for this mission and Neha had used unsuccessfully earlier. It was resting comfortably in the breast pocket of his shirt. He was looking at the boys; some rushing towards their dorms and some to the canteen for dinner. He shook his head. *Why the hell are they in engineering if they can't even work hard? I wonder how many of these are here because they were forced to take this a**hole's classes. If you can't stand up against difficulties and prove your mettle to the world what kind of engineer are you going to be?*

Gulati was sorting through some books on his table, looked at his wrist watch over and over.

Getting impatient is he?

'May I come in, sir?' asked Jackal said in a soft voice as he stepped under the doorway and clicked his pen once.

'Oh, Jai Kishan Amre, come in, come in. I've been waiting for you.'

He figured out my name?

'Come, sit,' Gulati gestured Jackal to sit next to him. He had placed a chair next to his. Like doctors have in their clinics.

He placed his hand on Jackal's shoulder.

'Come, sit next to me. Are you comfortable? Now you tell me, I have all the time in the world,' Gulati looked at him with a warm smile.

'Sir, now that you have given me such an honour to sit next to you and talk to you about my situation, I am really humbled.' Jackal touched Gulati's hand.

His touch made Gulati's eyes widen and Jackal heard him suck in a breath. *It is working.*

Jackal stealthily pressed the ringer button on the Nokia 1100 in his trousers pocket twice. The call would go through to the last dialled number, Ritesh's cell. A signal to him that the mood is set.

Right on cue, Professor Gulati's mobile rang, flashing 'Unknown number' instead of the digits.

They were using Rahul's cell. He had the money to have the network block his number from the public—very effective for their purposes since there was no way they could be traced.

Gulati was looking at Jackal's hand on his own. He had lifted his hand as if to place it over Jackal's, but in the end used it to answer his mobile.

He smiled at Jackal, 'Hello?'

Gulu gulu...gulu gulu...hey hey hey...bubub...bubub...hey hey...! The look of shock on Gulati's face was enough to show how freaked out he was. He cut the call and stared at his phone.

Jackal was trying hard not to grin.

The ghost of his haunting past back, Gulati looked a bit tense. He smiled at Jackal nervously.

After clearing his throat he said 'You were saying something?'

'Sir, I am an orphan from childhood. And the most misunderstood person. I think I am trapped in the wrong body and all the boys make fun of me. I am always very lonely sir,' Jackal woefully narrated the story they had fabricated story for Gulati's benefit.

'Trapped in the wrong body, means...you are...'

'I...I think so sir...' Jackal sobbed.

Even with his eyes screwed up with fake tears, he didn't miss the streak of joy that flashed on Gulati's face.

'Don't care about the world, be what you are, feel free and express yourself,' preached Prof. Gulati, pressing Jackal's shoulder. 'I understand your position. Look at me... I am...'

His mobile rang again. This time he answered after checking the screen, 'Unknown number... Hmmn...'

'Hello...'

Gulu gulu...gulu gulu...hey hey hey...bubub...bubub...hey hey...!

'Who is this bastard?'

The music continued. He cut the call.

'What happened, sir?'

'Nothing.'

'Can I be of some help, sir?' Jackal pressed Gulati's hand.

'No, not really. You say. What were you saying?' Gulati tried to flush the negative thoughts from his mind and concentrate on the job at hand in front of him.

'Sir, as I am entering into the final semester, I fear I will not get a good job, because the world outside does not want to believe that people like me...us...can work. I am afraid I will not get a job.'

There was a pause.

Jackal had thrown the bait in front of him. He touched the spy video pen kept in his breast pocket, an unconscious effort to check if it was working. *Come on say something.*

Gulati held himself back. He kept quiet, 'Hmm.'

His mobile started ringing again.

'Argh!' He picked up the mobile in his hand and started at it. 'Jai Kishan, I think we are getting late. You should go now. Meet me here tomorrow same time.'

He waved him out distractedly.

As Jackal hurried out of the room, he heard it.

Gulu gulu...gulu gulu...hey hey hey...bubub...bubub...hey hey...! Gulati had answered his phone again.

Professor Gulati's Quarters

Later That Same Night

Gulu gulu...gulu gulu...hey hey hey...bubub...bubub...hey hey...!

On my landline!!! Who is this bastard? I swear to God I will tear you apart, come in front of me!!

Gulu gulu...gulu gulu...hey hey hey...bubub...bubub...hey hey...!

The Next Day

How is this possible? Are they back? Gulati had had a sleepless night. Those chutiyas had been calling non-stop. Even putting his mobile ringer off had not helped. How does one put the landline on silent? After restlessly pacing his room and trying to block the noise with his pillows, he had thrown a chappal at the telephone; knocking it off the receiver.

The echoes of the song though still reverberated in his head.

After the tossing and turning excursion all night, he had woken up with a headache.

His lectures were also with the rowdiest classes today. Buggers had no concept of silence. Even walking through the corridors was a pain. Cell phones ringing all the time; kids screaming and shouting and playing music!

The only thing consoling him was that he will see Jai Kishan again tonight. What a beautiful soul this boy had. Oh he needed him so much. Poor boy. *I can ease his pain...*

His cell phone was burning up his pocket. The calls had started again in the morning. His phone was vibrating non-stop, making him feel cranky and irritable. He was drenched in fear of every incoming call. His reputation was again at stake, after so many years. He was the most respected and feared professor in the college. He had run the training and placement office with immaculate success for a decade. MSU was the most successful private university when it came to students getting placed. This is my power. I will see to them; those who dare try these stunts with me. *Who are they?*

Later That Evening

The engineering boys had done their due diligence. Tonight would be the end of this nexus.

Jackal wore a borrowed T-shirt, pink and a size just a tad too tight, the illusion of his choice of dressing to match his role. They were doing away with the spy pen tonight. The clarity they needed for recording the exchange today would come via the recorder. Neha had borrowed it from her classmate who recorded all the lectures in the device. The size of a match box, Jackal would have it in his jeans pocket, connected to an earphone lead with a mike, which would be strung around his neck. His phone too would be connected on a call with

Rahul's; who along with Ritesh would be stationed near the stairs. If the plan went as per their estimation, Rehan had a handycam ready to record their interaction, outside, near the hedges in the park.

At 8.00 p.m. exact, Jackal knocked on Professor Gulati's classroom door. He seemed to have ended his tuition classes early today.

Gulati heard the knock and rose from his desk. He too seemed to have dressed for the occasion. He was wearing a linen blazer and jeans today, the eyes behind his rimless glasses glinting under the lights. Jackal 'checked him out'; his eyes travelling from Professor Gulati's shoes upwards, to his shiny slightly ruffled white hair.

'Good evening, sir.'

'Good evening, Jai, come in.'

'You're looking very cool today, sir.'

'Oh...thank you, you are also looking handsome today.'

'Oh...thank you, sir,' Jackal said as he slowly walked towards the desk.

On cue, Ritesh dialled Gulati's landline.

The smile on Gulati's face was wiped off instantly. He picked up the receiver with trepidation.

'Hello...?'

'Hello? Hello? Who is this?' Gulati questioned. There was silence in the background. No music, no voice, nothing.

He looked at the receiver for a moment and placed it back on the holder.

'Let's go out. We'll walk and talk. Ah, good weather today, come on!' he motioned to Jackal as he rushed out of his office.

Jackal's surprised expression was fleeting. He thought it would take more calls than just one to get the professor outdoors! Haha! Their plan was working. As they fell into step near the stairs leading towards the ground, Gulati started, 'You were telling me something yesterday.'

Gulu gulu...gulu gulu...hey hey hey...bubub...bubub...hey hey...! The song played in the background.

Gulati turned around in shock.

'Wh...'

'What...what happened, sir?'

Gulati took a full turn, looking into the shadows. He couldn't find anyone. No source of the voice. No one.

'Did you hear that sound?'

'What sound? I didn't hear anything, sir.'

Oh...my mind must be playing tricks with me. Gulati shrugged off his irritation and concentrated on the boy in front of him.

'Leave it, you go ahead, tell me your problem?'

'Okay, sir, as I told you earlier, I am worried about my placements,' Jackal slowly started walking towards the nearby lamp post, 'and despite scoring well in exams I fear my personality and physical attributes will hinder my chances to get selected.' *Rehan will need the light, he must be recording this in the video camera.*

'Who said, being the way you are, will stop you from getting selected?'

'People in this world do not think the way you think, sir. I am really worried, sir' Jackal put his head in his hands.

Professor Gulati put his arm around Jackal. *Behind the camera, Rehan smirked. Brilliantly done, Jackal. He is pitching it right.*

Gulati seemed to quiver with the touch.

'I...Ah...I can make this easy for you Jai...I can confirm a job for you in the next placements.'

'Really, sir? You are so nice sir, how is this possible sir?' Jackal turned and held Gulati's other hand.

As Gulati started speaking, his mobile rang. He flinched, and brought it out of his pocket. The screen read 'Unknown number'. He took a deep breath and answered the call.

Gulu gulu...gulu gulu...hey hey hey...bubub...bubub...hey hey...!

'Motherf****r! Who are you?' Gulati snarled in a low tight voice. 'I will get you caught by police. I will get your ass kicked red. Stop calling me. You understand?' The line went dead.

Jackal placed his hands on Gulati's arm, 'Control your anger sir, it's not good for you.'

Furious as he was, Gulati sighed with Jackal's touch on his arm. He took a deep breath, and smiled at Jackal with affection, 'As I was saying, I can make things happen for you... Only if you be with me.'

'Be with you? I am with you sir?'

'I want you to be close enough to be my partner in...' before Gulati could finish the sentence his cell phone rang again. Fuming, he connected the call.

Gulu gulu...gulu gulu...hey hey hey...bubub...bubub...hey hey...!

'You son of a b***h,' he screamed, 'I am warning you for the last time, leave me, else I will kill you!' Gulati was shaking with anger.

There was silence on the other end. The song had stopped. '*Tu mere jhant ke baal bhi nahin ukhaad sakta,*' whispered a voice after a pause.

For the first time in years, Gulati heard his nemesis talk. He had a target to hit.

'You don't know me! I have the entire management of this university in my pocket. I know you are from this college only. I will chase you till the end of this world!' Gulati snapped, his face going red.

'Hahaha...you can't... *Tu mere jhant ke baal bhi nahin ukhaad sakta,*' the coarse voice replied from the other side.

Gulu gulu...gulu gulu...hey hey hey...bubub...bubub...hey hey...!

This time accompanied by maniacal laughter.

Gulati was staring at his phone in front of him with disbelief, the anger coming off him in waves. It was time for Jackal to prove his mettle, as a partner and queer lover. He needed to make Gulati fall for him, now. He walked the professor towards the bench in the park. He took the phone from Gulati's hands, the music still playing, and cut the call.

'Sir...why don't you have a seat?' Jackal insisted gently.

'This bugger doesn't know me, Jai Kishan! I have got everyone in this university in my pocket. I can crunch this c*****a any second,' Gulati snapped his fingers. 'I pay them a kickback for every paisa I earn through my coaching class. I pay them kickback for every student selected through campus in this university. This is all a business and it is created by a genius. I am the genius here.'

Jackal smiled. Gulati was confessing the crime and this time, it was all on tape.

'You are a genius, sir, you are a genius. Can you assure a job for me too, sir?' requested Jackal hopefully.

'I can do it immediately for you. I have connections in most of the companies,' Gulati offered with authority. 'Tell me which company you want to go to? Software, hardware anything. I take money from others to get them job in any of these companies but I can do it for free for you. Because I like you...I think, I love you Jai, I will take care of you,' he ended softly.

Jackal blushed, 'Ohh... I...ll...love you too, sir,' he got up and ran swiftly towards the darkness of the vast university campus, leaving a bemused yet confused Gulati behind.

As Rehan caught his expression on camera, from far away, a song started playing *gulu gulu...gulu gulu...hey hey hey... bubub...bubub...hey hey...!*

The Next Morning

I am a genius...
Mahesh R., a young boy from Karnataka in his second semester of Electronics Engineering saw the MMS video clip he had just received via Bluetooth on his phone. Professor Gulati was roaring about his achievements in setting up his business.

Hours later the video, which had been uploaded to the Internet, had gone viral. A big media furore erupted, demanding action against the corrupt teachers and management team involved in the scandal.

Professor Gulati was forced to resign the very same day, and along with him, the placement officers of the university.

The YouTube video created an uproar in the Indian corporate sector. Many companies started internal investigations. This sting operation made headlines across national dailies and media channels. Further investigations led to reports about the same nexus existing in other colleges around the country.

'India is now famous for being a country where capability and brilliance is bought over by money,' was the opinion in one of the leading English dailies.

Boys Hostel

A Few Weeks Later

The celebrations here had been quiet. Normal. Nobody wanted to bring attention to the real executioners of the revolution. It was decided to let the 'unknown caller' take all the credit. The boys had succeeded in their mission.

That afternoon during their exam preparation day-off, they had an unusual visitor.

'Ritesh,' said Pankaj Bhoj, knocked on Ritesh's open door.

Rahul, Rehan and Ritesh were surprised to see him here. They could see behind him, the rest of the hostellers had followed Pankaj and were in semi-circle around him.

'Thanks,' said Pankaj in a low voice looking directly at Ritesh.

'What?' questioned Ritesh, his eyebrows raised.

'I want to thank you for not dragging my name along with Gulati's.'

Ritesh looked at him for a few moments before walking up to him. 'What your friends did to Jackal...'

Pankaj interrupted Ritesh, 'About that, I'm sorry. I'll see to them. Tell Jackal I'm sorry.'

Ritesh looked back towards Rehan and Rahul and then at all the hostellers gathered behind Pankaj.

'Listen, there's a lot that has happened between us. I know Gulati used you as a pawn and gave you a backing, but you used that power in the wrong way. So, as long as you behave, only we will know the truth,' Ritesh indicated himself and his two friends.

'All we can offer right now is a truce. You're an intelligent guy; use your leadership for the good.' He offered his hand to Pankaj.

Pankaj was surprised by Ritesh's suggestion. Pankaj smiled at him as he shook Ritesh's hand in agreement to the terms. The crowd behind Pankaj Bhoj stared at them in surprise; they were expecting a great explosion between the two leaders of the packs at MSU. As Ritesh and Pankaj hugged each other smiling; the crowd behind them was stunned for a moment. Someone in the crowd broke the silence by whistling loud. What followed later was a round of loud cheers and claps, as both the leaders turned towards the crowd hand in hand. Rahul called Jackal and dragged him towards Pankaj who hugged him and apologized for what his boys has done to him. Jackal with a faint smile accepted his apology. Beyond that day, the animosity had all but disappeared between the two groups at MSU. The separatism was only fuelled briefly during sports matches and ragging; but never since then did it get as bad as 2005.

This was 3R's first revolution.

CHAPTER 10

December 2005

Winter descended heavy that year. December was a time for studying, project submissions, and preparations for the MBA or MTech entrance exams. The university had rushed about trying to calm the parents of their students that were worried about placements this year. The Dean had stepped in personally and was organizing the interviews himself. All bets were off, who'd get in and who not, now depended solely on their test marks and interviews.

The fourth year students had last two chances to make up for their slack in marks across the four years of engineering—the last two attempts to increase their CGPA. Joint studies became the norm, with day scholars and hostellers attempting to mingle and find new solutions to clearing their exams. There were two types of joint studies at MSU—one that involved using paper to write and learn, and one that involved rolling it up. The jury was still out on which method was more successful, although the one for least nervousness was awarded firmly and surely to the latter.

On one such night Rehan got an urgent call from his ammi. He was sitting with a bunch of his Mechanical classmates, copying and combining everyone's notes on Fluid Mechanics. A few moments later he ran into Rahul's room.

'I have to leave. I need to get to Bhiwadi.'

Ritesh got up and went towards Rehan who looked visibly sick, 'Now? What's happened? Is Rehana aunty okay? Abba?'

Rahul too was staring at Rehan with worried eyes, the crushed leaves in front of him forgotten. He stood as Ritesh forced Rehan down on his vacant chair. Rehan's ammi and abba were practically his only parental figures, he, their adopted son.

'Rehan? What is it? The exams...'

'I know. I know. I don't know what to do. I don't have a choice. Ammi just called. She sounded frantic. All I got was that abba has pneumonia and that it is bad, and I need to be there. You know them, if it wasn't serious, they wouldn't have called me. But I think it's something else...they're not telling me...'

'What about your preparations? Exams are starting next week,' piped up Jackal from the corner.

'I'm packing my books and other notes with me. I'll try to find time to study. Just pray that everything's okay...' Rehan said worriedly.

'Should we come with you?' asked Rahul.

'Nah bhai. I'll call if I need you.'

Rehan threw his books and a couple of shirts in a carryall and 20 minutes later he was boarding a Rajasthan Roadways bus to Bhiwadi. Ritesh had borrowed a bike from another hosteller and driven him to the bus stand on the highway.

Government Hospital

Bhiwadi, 2 a.m.

Rehan took an auto home from the bus stand at Bhiwadi, only to find the gate locked from the outside. He spoke to the auto rickshaw driver and requested to be taken to the Government hospital a few blocks away.

He found his father in a semi-private ward. The warden on duty had been handed a hundred rupee note for letting him in at this time of night and taking him to his father. His mother was dozing by the bed, on the rickety chair next to the bed. He went in quietly, hearing the wrecking coughs that were making his abbu tremble. As he neared, his abbu opened his eyes, as if he knew.

Rehan hurried to hold his hand, 'Abba...'

Rahim Khan grimaced as he squeezed his son's fingers. He felt his son's cool palm lovingly placed on his hot forehead and nudged his wife slightly, informing her of their son's presence. Rehana looked up groggily and saw her son in the pale shadows of the night, a reflection of her husband's youth. She went around the bed to where Rehan was and held him close. Rehan was immovable. He kept holding on to his father's hand. He only moved to bring the chair next to the adjacent bed closer to his father's and sat there the remainder of the night.

In the morning, the nurses and doctors came in for their daily rounds. As the duty doctor came by to check on Rahim, he enquired about the new addition at his bedside. The old gregarious man smiled at Rehan and told him it was good of him to be with his abba at this time.

After a while, once the doctor was done with the entire ward, Rehan followed him out and cornered him, 'Doctor sahib, please. You need to be honest with me. What is wrong with my father? Please. Please. I need to know.'

Dr Bharat looked at Rehan. He knew from his parents that he was in college, but with the worry etched in his young face, he looked like a little school boy.

'Okay okay. Come to my office.'

As Rehan closed the door to the sparse yet bright cabin, Dr Bharat pulled out a thick file and was waiting for Rehan to join him at his desk. Rehan looked perplexed with the fat looking file. He asked, 'Doctor, that's a big file. Is... Is that my dad's?'

Dr Bharat took a deep breath, 'Beta, I'm surprised your ammi and abbu haven't spoken about his illness with you, especially now.'

'I just got here last night...please. Tell me. This secrecy is...' pleaded Rehan.

'Rehan, its cancer. Your father has a form of leukemia. It's called multiple myeloma. It's a form of blood cancer. Rahim ji has had it for a while now. It was detected a few months ago, around August. He came in first with just the basic symptoms. He thought it was just exhaustion from working too much but Rehana ji insisted, I believe. It was detected early enough. It usually isn't lethal also. We had done all the tests and prescribed chemotherapy medicines also and for a while he was okay. He responded well to the medicines and was in remission, but last week he contracted pneumonia. Now, it's hard for his blood to produce the antibodies to fight the pneumonia and while we're doing everything we can, beyond a certain point we can't do anything. The infection has left him in a very weak state and the cancer has spread rapidly. We could have tried stem cell transplant, you would be required here to check the compatibility, but...'

Rehan's eyes moved between the doctor and the file, his expression one of disbelief as he stood up and rested his hands on the table, his head bent. He turned around and ran his hands through his hair, taking short strides across the cabin, from left to right and back again. The doctor remained quiet, observing a son coming to terms with his father's disease.

Rehan couldn't believe what was happening. He couldn't understand the enormity of what was ailing his father. *Why wouldn't they tell me earlier? There has to be a way.*

He stopped clenching his hair, looked up at the doctor and said in a defiantly hopeful tone, 'Which is the best cancer hospital in the country? Where is it? Mumbai? Delhi? Where? It's still not too late. Let's do this stem cell thing. Don't give up! You're a doctor! Don't give up. What... Where do I need to sign? Let's take him to the best hospital for cancer.' Rehan's words tumbled over each other, his fluster and agony channeled towards a goal, a mission to save his father.

Dr Bharat was shaking his head sorrowfully, 'Beta...'

'No doctor! Just tell me which hospital! And what is the procedure!!' Rehan exploded.

'Tata Memorial Hospital in Mumbai. It's a cancer specialty hospital. Rehan, we have already crossed that time. He's too weak to make the journey and that is if he can beat this pneumonia,' the doctor said softly, 'Why don't you go to your parents? They will want to be with you.'

Ya Allah raham!

Tears were streaming down his ammi's eyes as they both sat on the cold hard metal chairs in the hallway outside the ward. His usually strong and confident mother sat huddled in the chair next to him, his arm around her, as if to hold her up.

'Ammi, don't worry, we will take abba to Mumbai,' he said in a tight voice.

They had had an exhausting day. This afternoon after lunch, Rehan had quietly asked his parents why they hadn't told him anything earlier. He didn't know whether to be upset or mad about this. Why had they hidden it? He wasn't a twelve-year-old child.

Rahim Khan had in a weak, yet stern tone had told him to stop harassing his mother. They said they didn't want to disturb his studies and trouble him unless it was necessary. He was against calling him just before the exams also, but his mother and the doctors had insisted. They had even insisted that Rahim's younger brother and wife stay at home. Their children also had exams going on and if they were both at the hospital then the children's education would suffer.

Rehan was furious—at his parents for not calling him sooner, at his father for being ill, at the world and at God, for making his abbu sick. Now he was channeling all that anger into arranging for his dad to get shifted to Mumbai. He had been trying to connect with Tata Memorial to understand the procedure for transfer.

'But, how are we going to manage, jaana? We don't have that kind of money. A lot of it...a lot of it was spent on the hospital and chemotherapy medicines and tests. We...we won't be able...' ammi said hesitantly. She wanted to dissuade her son from raising his hopes too high.

Rehan cut her off, 'Ammi, don't worry about the funds. I will beg and borrow. Abba has a good respect here, lots of well-wishers, and our family. I know you have never asked mamu or chacha jaan for monetary help ever, but I will if required. They love abba. They will provide if necessary. Let me just find out how much first. Just...just don't lose hope.'

As he closed his eyes for the first time in over 40 hours, he thought about his father. Stern when required, but mostly loving and caring and a doting father, and a beautiful human being, Rahim Khan was a well-respected man in Bhiwadi and all his friends and family would pour in all possible help; money, extra working hands for support, anything. All he needed from Allah was time.

The sun was just about setting when Rahul and Ritesh walked into the hospital. Rehan was stepping out of the ward when he noticed them at the reception desk in the lobby. Rahul glanced his way and pulled Ritesh along with him.

'We got your text. What happened?'

—w—

Visiting hours were long over. Ritesh had taken ammi and gone to Rehan's house, all the while convincing her to rest for the night. Rahul and Rehan were sitting outside the ward. The doctors had given abbu medicines for the night, and the nurse would check on him around 2 a.m.

'Yaar, why is this happening? Why me?'

'Bhai...abbu will get better. You have your donor test tomorrow right? And your chachu is coming in too?'

'Yeah,' Rehan said, running his palms over his eyes. 'The doctors here are still unconvinced with the move. They say it's not going to be helpful...that we should wait and see if he gets better...'

Rahul put his arm around his friend, his brother for all intents and purposes. Losing abbu would be like losing his own father. In these four years, Rehana aunty and Rahim uncle were practically his surrogate parents. He couldn't bear for Rehan to go through the loss of a parent, like he had.

'Don't lose hope yet Rehan. Everything will be okay. You should get some rest. Do you want to go home? I'll stay with abbu.'

Rehan silently shook his head and leant forward, his head in his hands again.

Rahul had used his father's name and contacts the next day to speak to someone senior at Tata Memorial. After an in-depth explanation from their side, the hospital had asked for the reports of the tests and copies of the file be faxed or scanned and emailed to them. Rehan and his chacha's blood test results would be coming in the next day. And as they waited, they learnt the procedure of the transplant from their contact at TMH. She had told them that irrespective of the tests of the stem cells, they would have to wait for his father to get better.

'His immune system is very weak right now. He needs all his white blood cells and platelets to fight against the pneumonia. He needs to be strong for the chemo. And for stem cell radiation also, whether we use his own, his brother's or yours, one of the major side effects is low blood counts, which can lead to risks of serious infections and bleeding and in Rahim ji's case, his blood was already trying to fight an infection. We have no problem treating your father, Mr Khan, but you need to ensure that you are not worsening his condition by making him travel in such a state. You can try in the meantime to shift him to a private hospital. That might be better than where you are at the moment.' the medical counsellor had said in a soft yet firm voice.

Rehana, who was back at her husband's bedside looked refreshed. The rest at home had done her good. She had brought light homemade dal for Rehan's father, in the hopes that the homemade nutritious food would help him heal better. She had also brought stuffed paranthas for the boys. Ritesh was sitting with them while the other two had gone home to freshen up, after which they would find a private hospital to transfer Rahim to.

Ritesh was a kind boy, thought Rehana as he sat by the bedside. He kept indulging Rehan's father with funny anecdotes from college, about Rehan, about life and his parents and his plans for the future. How he sweetly kept saying he wanted Rahim and herself to be at all his life's events— graduation, his marriage when that happened. He told Rahim to get better and that after the exams he would take them for a holiday to Chandigarh.

She saw as Rahim's eyes slowly started closing, his medicines coming into effect. Sleeping this pneumonia off was the best solution for him. She quietly ran her hand over his forehead, checking to see if his temperature was still high and breathed a sigh of relief as he felt close to normal. She smiled at Ritesh when he realized that Rahim had fallen asleep. How lucky was her son to have found such friends in his life. Rahul and Ritesh were like sons to her. They were her three sons, the way they treated her. Rahul, the little lost boy who missed his mother so much, tries to be strong in front of the world. And look at them, all of them here instead of studying at college, preparing for their exams. She shook her head. She will send them all home to study when the other two come back. They can visit again in the morning.

Rehan and Rahul got back around seven. They had spoken to a hospital nursing home that was going to admit Rehan's dad. All four of them kept Rahim company during his visiting hours, after which Rehana adamantly told the boys to head on home, that they could take the morning shift while she went home to prepare some food.

'Rehana...' coughed Rahim father from the bed. 'I want to talk to our son. Wait for him outside.'

Rehan looked at his abbu with trepidation. *What was this about?*

'Beta... You are our noor. Do you know? Today I noticed how grown up you have become. I remember the boy we sent to college and here you are—taking responsibilities and helping your mother, organizing the hospitals. Whatever happens, Rehan, you have to complete your education okay? You should study and do well in your exams. Try and try and try again and be the best version of yourself. Never settle with yourself. Hard work, honesty and courage to face all odds, that is how life is to be lived. Everything else will follow...' The incessant coughing made Rehan uncomfortable.

'Baba, we can have this talk later also. You need to rest. Please. You shouldn't be talking so much. Your coughing gets worse.'

'No, Rehan. Now. What are your plans after college? *Socha hai aapne?* Job *ka*?'

'Ji abba,' Rehan held his father's hand.

'*Bataye.*'

'After college, actually *abhi*, after the exams, I will start preparing for the entrance exams for MS in USA.'

'Good. What will you do after your Masters degree?'

'Look for a job there itself. In America.'

'And then?'

'That's it. I will settle down there, earn lots of money and bring you and ammi to me. We will all live together there. Forever.'

'What will happen to Bhiwadi, your birthplace?'

'What...what will happen to Bhiwadi, abba?'

'Don't you owe something to this place, this nation?'

Rehan was taken aback, 'Abba, politicians are supposed to talk and act like this, not us middle-class people. There is nothing here for us.'

'So, you're going to give up on your country, your nation? Do you have no responsibility towards your homeland?'

Rehan answered calmly, 'Abba, why are we getting into this? What has the country done for us? Sure, I love India. But it is very hard making a life here. You yourself have worked so hard for all your life, what did you get? Nothing na? The world works on money. It is only the countries abroad that value your worth as a hard worker. Look at all the best Indian minds. They are who they are because they went to America or England to be someone.'

Rahim closed his eyes, with what looked like disappointment, prompting Rehan to ask, 'What happened, abbu? Are you okay?'

'Rehan...'

'No, abba, tomorrow!'

'Right now, Rehan. You will listen to me.'

'Do you think you don't have a responsibility towards this nation? A country is not made up of places and things; it is made up of people. You know as well as I, if everybody worthy contributed to this nation, it would become great. John F. Kennedy had said, "Ask not what your country can do for you, ask what you can do for your country." Rehan, you must take ownership of responsibilities. It is so easy to place the blame on someone else, wait for someone else to take the lead. Your generation has so many more opportunities and options than mine did. You have the backing of science and technology, of arts and humanities and the Internet. The world is your platter, why can't you serve it from your motherland? Why not start at grassroot level. Your house, Rehan, will only have a green garden if you water it daily. Why would you want to water someone else's garden and live there when yours has the same potential? Don't forget your roots. Every mighty tree has to have its roots firmly embedded in the ground. Be as big a man as you dream, the challenge would be to do it for your country. Rehan, I gave all I had to Bhiwadi. Because, I believe one day that this little city would be home to greatness. I gave everything I have to you too son. You will be my legacy to my city. I saved every penny of my income to make you an engineer, a really good one, one that you are becoming. Innovate, think and work for them that made you who you are Rehan… it is the biggest blessing and reward.'

Rahim's eyes bore into his son's and gripped his hands tight, willing him to understand, to think. The cough he had been repressing for long came bursting out. Rehan quickly picked up the glass of water on the bedside table and placed it to his lips.

'Abba, you are straining yourself. We can talk about this in detail when you are fit. Now please, sleep,' Rehan smiled and pulled the blanket on top of him, his face worried. Rehana who had walked back into the room hearing her husband's coughing fit had reached the bed. She took over Rehan's position and held onto her husband's hand.

'Go jaana, your friends are waiting. Go home and study. We'll see you in the morning.'

As Rehan bent and laid a kiss on his father's forehead, he heard a faint whisper, 'Think of what I said...'

—⚬—

They woke to a dull listless day and in Rehan's abbu's case, a lifeless morning. At half past five in the morning, Rahim Khan's heart stopped beating.

—⚬—

The local mosque had been informed; they took care of all the last rites as per the Islamic code. The community, neighbours, associates, friends and relatives had assembled at their home. Rehan was devastated—his father, his mentor in life had gone. All the emotions he had been repressing since arriving at Bhiwadi were wrecking him. Rahul and Ritesh knew he wanted to scream, to howl his anguish out, but kept stoic for his ammi's benefit. She was depending on him now. It was very difficult to hear Rehana aunty's agonizing wails. The ladies from the community were sitting with her as the final Janaazah prayers were being conducted. The house smelt of roses and incense sticks. Rahul and Ritesh were helping Rehan's chachi and moomani take care of the guests and arrange for food for all the guests. They arranged for a caterer to prepare food and refreshments for all those who came by to pay their last respects.

They looked at Rehan, sitting beside the motionless body of his father, his red eyes staring at his abbu. *He will get up anytime now, we spoke just last night.* Rehan's eyes were glazed over. His mind going over every insignificant moment he had spent with his father that today seemed to be worth his heart and his life. He recalled the ride to the annual fair on abbu's shoulders, of him cheering at the annual sports event, distributing sweets when he got selected in engineering college, of his plans after his college. So much left to do, so much life to be lived, so many conversations to be had...all those chances taken away.

Later that evening, a man came up to Rehan after paying his respects to Rehan's ammi, as they all stood in line near the entrance arch. He, in his business suit, introduced himself as Satyendra Chaudhary, the MD of Mahadev Industries. He handed his card over to Rehan and gripped his folded hands in his own large ones.

'Rehan beta, your father spoke of you often, and was very kind and helpful and a very very good friend of mine. He is irreplaceable. His loss will be felt forever. Come meet me after you finish college. My doors will always be open for you.' Rehan looked at him and bowed his head in gratitude. Satyendra Chaudhary placed a hand on his head in blessing and headed out.

Ritesh and Rahul stayed with Rehan for the next three days, during his period of mourning. The three boys, though they tried to study on ammi's insistence, kept themselves enclosed in what used to be abbu's study—the small quiet room he used for his prayers and kept his collection of books, his poetry and religious books and memorabilia from the years gone by. The boys kept recalling stories of their previous visits with Rehan filling them in on long forgotten stories from his childhood.

They were going to be travelling back to university tomorrow morning. They had all missed one exam each already, but would reach back in time for the rest of them.

Most of the guests had gone back by now, with only a few stragglers remaining. People from all over had poured into their house over the three days, to pay their respects to the family; neighbours and the community members kept dropping by with food. Rehan felt overwhelmed to observe just how well respected and loved his abbu had been in this city.

Today was their last evening at home. Rehan had spent the day at his mother's side. He felt like he was floating, adrift in the middle of the sea with no anchor. He looked at his ammi, imagining she felt the same. She looked like the life force had been sucked from her, but even in her weakness, there was strength in her. The next three months would be a time for her to recuperate. Rehan's moomaani and chachi were going to alternate being with her during her time of iddat, since she wouldn't be able to step out. It was only his ammi and him now; just them against the world.

They were all sitting in the open courtyard, enjoying the last few days of the wintery sun, Rehan's head in his ammi's lap. She was running her palm on his forehead softly, as he stared at her. She smiled down at him, looking into her husband's eyes.

CHAPTER 11

March 2006

MSU's engineering batch of 2006 spent their last semester lounging around in their college campus. The university was busy figuring out placements, and the fourth years used their time to study for further entrance exams—some for their Masters, some leaving engineering completely and opting for an MBA and switch career choices.

On one such slow weekday morning in March, the boys were smoking up on the rooftop of one of the buildings.

'What are you so quiet about dude?' Jackal asked Rahul, looking at his glum expression.

'Neha. It's her bir...' started Rahul.

'Yeah. Birthday girl is absent today,' Jackal said nonchalantly.

'I've been looking for her. Wait, how do you know?'

'Well, I have my sources.'

'We need to know where her house is,' Rahul said firmly, making rings of the smoke he was blowing out.

'What will you do with that information Romeo?'

'I can't wait. I have to tell her that I love her. It'll be her birthday present,' Rahul winked in response to Jackals question.

'So, you are going to enter her house, and tell her you love her in front of her family?' Jackal grinned.

Rahul kissed Jackal on his shining bald temple, 'What a great idea, let us go do exactly that!'

'You are one hell of a crazy f****r, last time your heropanti dive to win the race left you with bruises all over your body,' Jackal backed away.

'Shut your mouth, you will come with me else I will tell the whole world who leaked on the Blue Bull night.'

Jackal's face turned sour, 'You always blackmail me Rahul.'

New Friends Colony, Delhi

'I can't believe you still ride this antique piece of shit,' said Rahul as he got off and brushed the dirt off his shirt and stretched. The old, rickety Moped came to a dead sputtering stop a few feet short of Neha's bungalow.

'Hey, don't disrespect my ride. She's been very faithful to me,' Jackal replied even as he tried to restart the red scooter.

'I can't believe I didn't get my Thunderbird repaired. I'm such an idiot. I should have got it sent to the garage back when it got stalled. Didn't realize I'd need it. Arrgh!' Rahul shoved his fingers through his hair in frustration. He whipped out a cigarette and lit one to calm himself, as he glanced nervously at the white bungalow.

He looked at Jackal huffing and puffing, dragging his scooter to the side of the road, murmuring sweet words to it in the attempt to bring it back to life. He shook his head, 'I'm calling for a car to be sent here. Don't know if your "love" will make it back to college.' He called home and gave the driver the address to Neha's house.

She lived in what seemed to be a quaint little multi-storeyed bungalow. He could see the tip of the slanted white roof and balcony. Neha had mentioned there was a lawn where she used to enjoy playing with her cousins when they were younger. The house was enclosed within vine covered high boundary walls and to one corner was a huge wrought iron gate. A middle-aged guard had stepped out of his cabin just inside the gate and was looking at them through the small grilled window on the gate.

'What?' he questioned Rahul.

Rahul quickly stepped on to the half-smoked cigarette and stubbed it out.

'*Bhaiya, Neha ji se milna tha...*'

'*Baby ghar pe nahi hai.* Go away,' the guard said, looking Rahul up and down, and glancing at the scooter they came on.

'Bhaiya, can you tell her it's Rahul from her college?'

'*Arre*,' he seemed to get flustered as he looked at Jackal's appearance behind Rahul. '*Bola na*. She's not here. *Bohot aate he tumhare jese.* Chalo. Run away now.'

He walked back into his small cabin and slammed the door shut.

Rahul looked back at Jackal and then the house and walked towards the scooter dejected. *This is not happening.*

―⚋―

Ten minutes later, the guard heard someone banging on the gate. He stepped out and clutched his heart as he saw who it was at the gate.

'Wwwhat do you want?' he stammered.

'Uncle ji, some help?' requested Jackal in his wheezy tone, pointing to his scooter.

'Where has your friend gone?'

'He went to find a mechanic,' Jackal said. 'Can you please help me lift the moped? *Gir gayi.*'

The guard opened the gate and stepped out, walking cautiously towards the fallen scooter.

Twelve metres away, on the other side of the bungalow, Rahul was climbing up the vines. He knew a bit of parkour from his school days, dabbling in it in college. Putting those skills at work, he took a leap towards a nearby tree, leveraging himself up towards the top of the boundary wall. *Thank God, they didn't have any glass shards over the top. That would have been fun.* He heard Jackal engage the guard in a louder than his normal tonality. This gave him approximately thirty seconds to get off this wall, cut across the lawn and find and then get to Neha's room. *There's no way I'm leaving without seeing her today!* He dropped to his feet and sprang up quickly, running to the side behind some trees, away from the glass floor to ceiling windows.

Neha had once said she loves watching the sun rise from her balcony. Crossing his fingers he looked at the sky, wishing for luck and took a flying leap up the water pipe. He started climbing as he latched on and jumped to the balcony from there. He swung his legs up and vaulted over the railing. He could hear the latest hit song 'Hips Don't Lie' by Shakira, playing from the first out of two rooms on the balcony, its door slightly ajar, the sheer white curtains swaying softly with the wind. *This has to be hers.*

He quickly brushed his hair back off his forehead and wiped his dirty hands on his jeans. Bringing the sling bag he had on to the front, he extracted two gift wrapped boxes. Holding them delicately in one hand, he pushed open the door.

Neha was seated at the dressing table, wearing what could be described as a really sexy top—it looked like a fancy bandage covering half her torso with matching teeny tiny shorts. He was dumbstruck.

Neha saw Rahul's reflection in the mirror and jumped up. 'What the hell, Rahul! What...how did you get here?'

He gaped at her, his jaw on the floor.

On seeing his expression, she grabbed a sheer nightgown from the back of the chair and put it on.

'Close your mouth Rahul! How on Earth did you get up here?' Neha quickly ran to the open balcony window and peeped outside to check if anyone noticed him get in. As she shut the door, she turned to see him looking at her sheepishly.

He whistled.

She blushed.

'I came to wish you a happy birthday, princess,' Rahul held out the two presents in his hand.

'Oh! Ahh... Thanks!' Neha giggled in surprise and walked towards him slowly and took the gifts from his hand.

She raised herself up on to her tip toes, leant forward and whispered in his ear, 'I'm a queen, not just a princess,' and pushed him back playfully.

Rahul grinned. *Oh God! She's hot! Sweet and playful and a queen. All in one.*

She sat down on her bed and put the gifts to a side, 'So, are you always this filmy or are you treating me special?' she said pointing towards her balcony. 'Are you *Kuch Kuch Hota Hai*'s Shahrukh Khan? Really?' she looked at him with a coy, challenging smile.

Rahul threw his head back and laughed.

'*Kya karun Janeman! Kuch kuch hota hai...tum nahi samjhogi!*' Rahul imitated the infamous god of Bollywood romance and promptly did his signature pose.

Neha too burst out laughing and threw one of the many cushions from the bed at him, 'You're horrible.'

'You know if daddy finds out you're here, he'll cut you up and throw you to the dogs?' Neha looked at him, wiping her eyes delicately from laughing too much.

'Hahaha, that's okay. You're worth it. Are you going to open those gifts sometime today babe?'

She looked at him coyly. 'Sure.'

Rahul dragged the dresser chair toward the bed and sat facing her, watching her unwrap what he got her.

'Oh! This is...it's very pretty,' said Neha as a beautiful small chain fell into her hands as she opened the first box. It was a customized bracelet with beautiful tiny Swarovski charms all over it. She held it up to look at them closer. There in miniature form was everything that depicted their relationship so far—a car, a bike, the sun, a tiny running shoe, a jacket, a cupcake, a rose and a heart.

She blushed, 'Rahul...'

'The car and bike for the first time I ever saw you, on the highway towards college, the running shoe, is of course the Nehru Park incident, the sun when we took that walk in the park, our first real conversation, and the next one is a reminder of that time when you had worn my jacket in the hostel...' he eased off.

Neha was looking at the bracelet, seemingly at a loss for words, she whispered, 'and the next three?'

'Ahh well, why don't you open your next gift?'

Neha laughed and tore into the box in her lap. Inside there was a single piece of plastic carton containing a chocolate cupcake and a single rose.

'Happy Birthday, Neha,' Rahul moved forward, his knees touching hers. He picked up the cupcake and held it out to her.

'It smells good.'

'I made it for you,' Rahul grinned.

Neha laughed, 'Oh so you want to poison me on the day I turn 20?'

'Haha! Sure. Kill you with love maybe. Let's cut this for you?' Rahul took out a candle and lit it with a lighter. Bringing it closer to Neha, he said, 'Make a wish, beautiful.'

Neha smiled at Rahul's charm, she shook her head grinning at his antics.

'Happy Birthday to you,' Rahul sang the birthday song and she blew the candle and closed her eyes. He took the opportunity to kiss her slightly on her cheek.

Neha laughed out loud, 'Rahul Bhatia!'

He removed the candle and held the cake up for her.

'Do you need permission to feed me my birthday cake?' she raised her eyebrows with a naughty grin.

This had Rahul blushing too. He put the cupcake to her lips. She moved her mouth to the side, and took a bite close to where his fingers were holding the cake, managing to bite his finger in the process.

She winked at him as he cried out.

'That was for barging into my room,' Neha managed to say with her mouth full of cake and eyes brimming with laughter. Rahul smiled and looked at her childlike enthusiasm.

'So, good or what?'

'You're right...tastes like you've made it!'

'Did you like it?' asked Rahul.

'Tell me what the most important ingredient in this cake is?'

Rahul laughed, stumped, and came up with the most logical answer he could think of, 'Sugar?'

Neha went into peals of laughter.

'Hey! What about me?' He asked as she went in for another bite.

'You want a bite too?'

'Oh yes!'

Neha held the cupcake with her lips and used her fingers to call Rahul closer, his eyes wide.

He brought his lips to the cake. They were one bite away from a proper kiss.

He couldn't believe his luck.

They both broke off a piece each of the cake and had a tiny bite left when Neha suddenly pulled back, wrinkling her nose.

'You've been smoking again! You know that shit stinks na!'

'I ah...no...ah... It was Jackal...I didn't...'

'Oh! Did you kiss him after he smoked, liar! Hahaha,' Neha playfully swatted Rahul as she stood up and laughed. Rahul pushed his chair back too and held her close, both of them laughing in each other's arms.

The door of the room opened, unnoticed by either of them. It was Mrs Khare's shocked voice that brought them back to reality.

'What's going on?'

'Sir, it is not what you think it is,' said Rahul in a low tone his head bent down.

He had been escorted down by a stern looking Mrs Khare. She was livid. She frogmarched him down after directing her daughter to wear something decent and join them in the living room downstairs.

Dr Khare and Neha's mother were now seated on the plush leather sofa facing him. He was standing in the centre of the room looking down at his feet. Neha's younger sister, Nisha, too, had come downstairs listening to the commotion and was grinning while sitting on the side chair, her feet tucked under her.

Neha ran downstairs in her favourite pair of jeans and stood next to Rahul, 'Papa, it's not what ma thinks.'

Neha's mother looked at her sternly and ordered her to sit on the sofa to the side, away from Rahul.

'You, young man have been trespassing in our house. How dare you get into Neha's room without permission? Who are you? What is the meaning of this disrespect? You just wait. I will call the police station and have you arrested.'

Dr Khare picked up a cordless phone and pressed 9—for the guard room apparently. Two minutes later the middle-aged guard ran in and went still with shock seeing Rahul inside the house.

'You?! How...sir, *main police ko janta hun. Mein abhi phone karta hoon.* He had come earlier. I'd made him run away! How did he get in?'

To the even further surprised looks on Neha's parents' face, Rahul responded, 'You will not call the police, sir, I know it.'

'What do you mean?' Dr Khare got up. Rahul could see where Neha got her demeanour from—the same staunch stance, the flare of the nostrils, and mostly the eyes; those eyes spitting fire. Neha was just a smaller, more beautiful but yet as tough version of her father.

'Because as tough as you look, sir, you are a kind and compassionate man too. Twenty years ago you opened a small dispensary by taking only ₹10 as your fees when your colleagues took a minimum ₹50 from patients. You offered your services free to poor children and slowly you became the messiah of the children of all auto drivers and needy people in Delhi. God reciprocated your kindness with extreme grace and you were hailed as one of the richest and most respected child specialists in this country. With all that history of caring behind you, I'm certain you won't wrong anyone intentionally. I, too, am a man of my words sir, therefore, when I said, we weren't doing anything wrong, I can assure you, Neha and I were only talking,' Rahul advocated.

Dr Khare seemed to be stumped by this impressive speech. Neha shook her head. *Oh! What a smartass.*

'It doesn't change the fact that you sneaked up to her room! You disrespe...'

'I apologize for the disrespect, sir, ma'am. I did come by the front door, but was sent away. I really couldn't have gone back without meeting Neha on her birthday.'

'Hmmm, you study with her in college? Are you her class fellow? What does your father do?' he changed the topic.

'Yes, sir. But I'm her senior. Last year. Will be graduating in the summer. My father has a steel business,' Rahul replied.

Dr Khare shook his head, 'Young man you should concentrate on your studies. Be a good engineer, work hard, get a good job and help your family live a better life. Now is not the time for this,' he placed his hand on Rahul's shoulder and started to move him along.

Rahul looked confused. *Better life?*

In that instance, he understood, Neha's dad was under the impression that he was from a needy family, because he knew all about his charitable work.

He shook his head slightly in quiet laughter just as his mobile started ringing.

He brought out his phone, which much to the surprise of Dr Khare was the latest and most expensive model of Blackberry.

'Excuse me, sir.

'Ji Ram Singh ji. Come to F-143.'

The guard had rushed forward to open the gate for his boss. The three of them saw Jackal waiting outside in front of the gate, walking nervously from left to right; the antique moped lying on the side near the entrance.

Dr Khare looked confused. Between doing double takes from Jackal's appearance, the rusty old moped and Rahul's Blackberry, he missed the Mercedes SUV come to a standstill in front of the house.

A uniformed chauffer stepped out and ran to Rahul's side.

'Good evening, baba. I have got the car for you. Will you be coming home for dinner?'

'Not today Ram Singh ji. Thank you. Can you please take Jackal's bike and get it fixed? Get it sent to the college when it is okay.'

'Ji, baba,' Ram Singh went to get the keys from Jackal and stood to the side.

Dr Khare and the guard looked flabbergasted, their gaze travelling from the SUV to Jackal, to Rahul and the driver.

He looked at Rahul curiously.

Rahul, as he walked towards the open door of the 4x4, turned around and faced Neha's father, 'Thank you again, sir, for not calling the cops. Wish your daughter a happy birthday once again and good day to you.'

As he drove off, he looked once towards the house and saw Neha standing just inside the gate. He nodded at her as she smiled.

Dr Khare turned towards the driver and said, '*Ye kaun the?*'

'*Rahul baba? Rajesh Bhatia ji ke bete. Unki company hai na, Bhatia Steel Pvt Ltd.*'

Ram Singh turned away, brought out a Nokia 1100 and called for the mechanic.

―⁂―

Dr Khare got the guard to shut the gate again and walked back in, his hand at his graying goatee. He looked at Neha standing there and said, 'He's the son of one of the richest man in Delhi today! And you like him? Or, well, he likes you?'

Neha looked at her dad impassively.

He shook his head with a look of ecstatic disbelief and walked in, leaving Neha surprised...

She got off easy and her dad met Rahul and she was still alive. *Haha.*

CHAPTER 12

—⁂—

The winds blowing through the university hilltop had changed its direction. The westerly winds were feverish and bought with them the indication of the change. These hot winds during the beginning of April catapulted the exam fever in the students. The campus was unusually quiet, fewer number of students could be spotted wandering. Library was full of bent heads and essential books emptied from shelves.

An old ceiling fan rattled in a room on the first floor of C wing of the boys' hostel. Rahul slammed his book shut, *TV & Radar Engineering,* and burst out in exasperation, 'Who the hell wrote this book? It's bullshit.'

Rehan looked up in surprise from his position on the sofa and shook his head. He had his fingers in his ears and had been religiously chanting extracts from his Machine Design theory.

Ritesh who had been leaning back in his chair, reading through his notes on Web Engineering, laughed. He too shut his book and took his earphones out of his ears. Even listening to Alt-Rock while studying hadn't helped. They just wanted to get out of the college. To get on with their lives.

They both watched as Rahul flopped down on the bed theatrically and announced he would have loved being in a movie theatre with Neha right about now, but was instead wasting his time with Delay Line Cancellers, '*Life hi cancel ho gayi he meri!*'

Ritesh laughed. He pushed back his long tresses behind his ears and said sagely, 'Hero, this is the finale. Along with the five subjects in this semester, we have one extra paper from last time to do. We need to work hard.'

Rehan looked up at them and understood the lecture was aimed specifically at Rahul, who looked completely disinterested.

'I am only wishing right now. I know how important it is for me to escape from my dad and the family business. I want to get any f*****g job outside Delhi and live alone peacefully.'

'Rahul, you are in some ways a lucky guy. Many would have given their right arm to get the silver spoon you were born with,' Rehan said thoughtfully.

'Bhai, I know...but everything comes at a cost. Mine was too heavy to pay. That's why I want to get out.'

Ritesh interjected and said, 'Guys, let's take a break. This assoholic fan also isn't helping. Maybe they have the AC on in the canteen. Let's go take a look. Get something to eat?' He looked at his two brothers, so close yet on opposite ends of the spectrum. Rahul would happily give up everything for Rehan's family support and Rehan wanted to work like a dog to get to Rahul's status. Their different ideologies and ways of looking at situations would evolve into philosophical banter much like two parallel ships on a never-ending journey. Rahul with his carefree way of looking at things and relying on how his gut felt at that moment, whereas Rehan had a more meticulous and calculated approach toward situations. Ritesh would often be the mediator for them, his approach balancing both intuition and instruction.

The trio walked into the relatively cooler atmosphere of the canteen 10 minutes later. They picked up a Thums Up each and found their way to their reserved table. As Ritesh was crossing the small LCD screen on the pillar, he noticed the ticker of a popular news channel.

ASHOK CHAKRA FOR MAJOR ASHOK RAJWARDHAN, BIHAR REGIMENT/51, SPECIAL ACTION GROUP, POSTHUMOUSLY AWARDED FOR A SUCCESSFUL COUNTER INSURGENCY OPERATION.

His feet seemed rooted to the floor as he heard out the entire news item. Rahul called him over from the table. 'What's up, dude? Ritesh!'

'Oh! What? Yeah, I'm coming,' Ritesh snapped out of his reverie and headed to the table. 'This stuff is so inspiring. My God! I am so proud of this guy right now. His sacrifice makes me love my country even more.'

Rehan and Rahul too turned towards the TV to see what was happening.

'I have filled out the admission form to join the Army under the University Entry Scheme'.

Rehan and Rahul both cricked their necks as they turned back around really quickly at Ritesh's announcement.

'Bro, Army? Why?' Rahul asked.

'Why not?' enquired Ritesh, raising his brow whilst pushing his long hair back again.

'I mean, who joins the Army nowadays? They pay you peanuts. They don't value the intelligence of the individual. You join the ranks and just follow dumb orders. You get postings at the weirdest of the places, no time for family or a personal life. It sucks! With your ability you can easily crack a good result in all competitive exams and get a super awesome corporate job and chill for the rest of your life,' Rahul advised.

'I am chilled out serving the nation. By joining the force

I'll be able to serve the society; to be able to give back to my country, my people,' Ritesh replied with a calm smile.

'Earn money and give back to the society you so care about Ritesh. You're becoming such a cliché. All this "giving back" stuff seems attractive when you are young and the rush of adrenaline drives your decision. Once the storm of this chemical stops inside you, you grow old, you become a family man then you realize you could or should have made a better choice in youth,' interjected Rehan.

'Guys, I get where you're coming from. All I can say is "to each his own". Did I try and convince Rahul to stay back with his family and help fulfil his father's dream of expanding the business? He wants to escape, fine, let him do that. At least he is following his heart. In the process so what if he is breaking the heart of his loved ones?' Ritesh retorted.

Rahul looked at Ritesh with surprise trying to catch the meaning hidden in his words.

'And look at you, Rehan, your father wanted you to be in Bhiwadi, but you're still keen on going to the US. If you ask me what I think you should do, I'd say, follow your heart. Follow your heart and it will lead you to the right path. Align your mind with what your heart says, or vice versa and you'll never regret one second of your life. And that's what I am doing,' Ritesh finished and leaned back, tilting his chair, as was his signature style.

After a short reflective silence, Rahul piped up, 'It's dangerous dude, you can get killed also.'

'We're one breath closer to dying every time we breathe, bro. This country is worth dying for!' Ritesh said. *It's worth dying for...*

AIIMS, Delhi

Present Day, 11 October 2011, 12.30 a.m.

Ritesh's words echoed inside Rehan's head. He had finally reached AIIMS. The hospital was flooded with people, even at this time. Rehan hated hospitals, avoided them since he lost his father—they made him choke, the anxiety building on the fumes of phenyl and that sickly medicinal smell. He quickly found his way to the ICU. Rahul had reached 10 minutes earlier and texted him where to come.

The patient visiting hours were long over. *I guess my friend deserves the special permissions being awarded to him. If only they weren't in this situation.*

Rehan saw Rahul sitting hunched on one of the chairs outside the ICU hall. As he walked up to his brother, he called out. On seeing Rahul's moist eyes, Rehan was a little taken aback. He had never seen Rahul break down. Rahul on seeing Rehan walking towards him, got up and paced towards him. Both the friends gave each other a hug which was more of a consolation to each other in this tough time. Rahul looked at Rehan and said, 'I can't lose him too. Can't lose my mother and my brother.'

Rehan set his bag down, 'What did they say? How is he? Where are aunty and uncle?'

'The docs won't tell me anything, but uncle met me. They've just gone back to sit with the director of his agency. Apparently, the impact from the fall and the internal injuries from the blast are very serious. He is in a critical condition for the next 24 hours. He's been doing well for the last two hours though; showing signs of recovery. He just got out of surgery a while ago, apparently. He's a fighter though, that's what they're saying,' Rahul responded with a croaky voice.

Rehan looked up and sent a *shukrana* to God, as he put his arm around Rahul and said, 'We're talking about Ritesh here! He has more GMD than all of us put together. He will win. He'll…he'll make it.'

Both sat quietly in the eerie silence of the room. The only sound was that of a thick drop of water from a tap hitting repeatedly the metallic base of the washbasin installed in one corner of the lobby. There was nothing more to do, than sit and wait it out. They were exactly where they had to be…

Rehan broke the silence after a while, 'Do we know anyone else in Delhi, who'll be here?'

'Neha,' Rahul whispered a name he only said out loud in his dreams now.

'Oh, have you spoken to her?'

Rahul scoffed slightly, 'You still remember the farewell night?'

2006

Six Years Ago, Farewell

You only live twice, once during 'freshers party' and another during 'farewell party'.

The motto at MSU.

With immense fanfare, frivolous grandeur and a nostalgic camaraderie, the farewell week was one crazy frenzy of secret parties, official ones and culminations of love and lust for a lucky few. The central auditorium had been decorated to its best, the standard lights and fixtures increased to give it a magical feel. Tonight, was the official farewell party, for which day scholars had special permissions to stay back at the hostel for the night. Professors dressed in their usual formal suits and saris were crowded around the buffet area. Their idea was to let kids be kids. A few seniors came up every once in a while to chat with the professors, some to apologize for their antics over four years, and some to say thanks and create network. The last four year of togetherness formed the core of most of the discussions and jokes throughout the night. Amongst other things, the juniors had prepared skits, mimicry items and songs to entertain their seniors, for one last time. Since everyone was dressed in their formal Indian best—glittering saris and well-cut sherwanis, they'd staged a fashion show competition between the senior batches across the engineering divisions; the titles of best dressed, best walk and all-rounder personality would be awarded.

The juniors knew they couldn't let their seniors off without a proper send off. Alcohol and joints were snuck in. A secluded, cordoned off laboratory on the top floor, leading to the terrace was chosen as their theka. They'd arranged for rum, both dark and white, and some drinks. Anything and any combo went, as long as it was masked by the fizzy drink, so that the professor's don't find out. The juniors were pouring the alcohol into pet bottles and topping up everyone's glasses. If someone wanted to smoke up, they had to collect from the lab and walk on to the roof.

Some partook it to celebrate the end of an era, some to gain liquid courage to let loose this night. Ritesh, Rehan and Rahul had their glasses topped off a couple of times now and were chilling, overlooking what had been their kingdom for the almost four years.

Rahul's mobile buzzed. It was a text from Neha.

Hey U! :)
'Sup?
U temme?
V r partyin
Miss me? ;)
Ofcrs. Wish u wr here
:) Wish granted

Rahul looked up from his cell and as if the crowd parted magically for them at this moment, and the music changed to a slow romantic number. *Fate was truly on his side tonight.*

Rahul considered himself lucky as he watched the girl of his dreams walk towards him, wearing a glittering short black dress. It moulded her figure like she was poured into it. Her hair was swept to one side and seemed extra shiny and straight today. Those legs he was crazy about, seemed longer than usual, the illusion offered by her five inch pencil heels.

'Wow, you look gorgeous!' Rahul said as Neha walked up to him.

'I thought of giving you a surprise. Nitin sir, from third year who arranged the party is a friend of sorts. He stays close to my place, we carpool sometimes. I asked him to let me come in today since most first and second years are not invited. He obliged, gladly,' Neha winked at him.

'Understandably, who would refuse a chick as hot as you for a party?'

'Shut up,' Neha laughed and punched him lightly on the shoulders.

'Let's dance,' Rahul laughed.

He was dragging her onto the dance floor even as she started nodding. Her trail of laughter followed them as they disappeared between the crowds dancing near the DJ's console.

A little while later, they extracted themselves out of the mesh of dancing figures and walked towards Ritesh and Rehan who were laughing while watching Jackal attempt his version of a mix of Jitendra's and Mithoon's dance steps, a few extra drinks down. Both the boys exclaimed in delight on seeing Neha there and welcomed her with those sideway hugs reserved for bhabhis.

As the song changed, Rahul dragged Neha back to the edge of the DJ setup. Ritesh and Rehan watched them go, happy for their friend. *He looks so thrilled.*

One of their juniors signalled to Rahul to come upstairs for lighting up the joint. They wanted to make it a ceremony, 'senior's passing the joint to the juniors,' both literally and figuratively. Rahul excused himself from Neha and left her in the 'custody' of his brothers. He was happy tonight. Neha, made him feel loved, special. He finally just wanted to be with one girl, and this realization made him ecstatic. When he reached the rooftop, all his juniors had formed a circle and were waiting for him to 'puff, puff, pass'. He laughed at the symbolism of it. The boys had arranged for a bottle for a toast. Someone brought out shot glasses and the group exchanged some smooth amber whisky shots. Rahul, being the coolest senior, was offered three in quick succession. He downed them in celebration of his life tonight. After spending 20 minutes chilling with the boys, he made his way back downstairs to Neha.

Neha, Ritesh and Rehan were watching the one-man show that Jackal was headlining. The other dancers were giving

The Amigos

him a wide berth. His dance skills were cracking everyone up. Jackal went from snake charmer, to a snake, then a bhangra king and finally a break dancer. Neha was in splits watching Jackal dance, loving the freestyle vibe from Jackal, who danced like he didn't give a care to the world.

'I need to apologize to the poor guy; I wasn't very nice to him in the beginning,' Neha reminisced as she told Ritesh and Rehan about her first encounter with him in Nehru Park, leaving them holding on to the table for laughing so hard.

'He is a sweet soul,' she admonished, holding back her laughter.

'There are sweeter souls here?' Rahul enquired, as he wrapped his arms around Neha from behind her.

She smiled and leant back against him. He whispered in her ear, 'Let's go for a walk, I need to tell you something.'

They held hands as he walked her out to the corridor and up the stairs leading towards the open windows of the deserted first floor.

'Where did you go in between?' asked Neha.

'Oh, some kids wanted to have a word with me,' Rahul avoided telling her exactly what he had been up to, she used to freak out about just plain smoking.

After a few seconds of silence, he asked, 'Why did you come?'

Neha looked up at him, 'Here or to the party?'

'Both.'

'Well, I wanted to be a part of your special day. Help make it sweeter!' she winked.

He held her hand up to his lips and kissed it slightly.

'Thanks.'

As Neha giggled nervously, Rahul said, 'And what about here?'

'Well, I was tired of standing in one place. Like this I'd get some fresh air, and…you're good company,' she laughed and stuck her tongue out at him.

Rahul looked down at her and felt a zing of energy pass through him. He grabbed her face and kissed her, slowly and lightly at first. He wanted their first kiss to be a proper one; one that she remembered. She moaned slightly as they kissed in the secluded hallway, with the music thumping in the distance and moonlight shining in on them. *It was perfect.*

Rahul felt her hands on his chest, and he moaned. He stepped forward, lips still intertwined, and pushed Neha against the wall. He plundered her mouth with his tongue and kissed her savagely, his lips smashing against hers. He pressed his body against her, making her feel exactly what she and this kiss were doing to him. He was so hard. As reflex action he started grinding against her, his hands moving over her body.

He suddenly registered that Neha was pushing him. Those noises she had started making were not moans of ecstasy…her lips were shut, tight. He moved his face back to see her.

In that instant, Neha slapped him.

Hard.

'How dare you?' Neha shouted at him as she pushed him back and herself away from the wall.

'What the hell do you think of yourself? Of me?' she screamed at him, furious.

'I love you,' Rahul said, confused. 'I just wanted to show…'

'No, what you were doing was taking advantage. All you showed me was what an a**hole you are!' Neha was livid; she turned around and started walking towards the stairs, leading to the party.

Rahul ran to her and caught her arm.

'N...N... Neha, no. Wait...just wait,' Rahul stammered, his drinks and joints catching up on him, although he believed it was Neha, who made him high.

Neha freed her arm from his grasp, 'For what, Rahul? For you to force yourself on me again? No, thanks. Why don't you go drink and smoke up some more?'

'I... I wasn't...' Rahul started, trying to hold on to her.

'Don't f*****g lie to me Rahul. You stink. Stay away from me,' Neha turned around and started down the stairs.

'Neha...'

'Don't,' Neha looked back at him and held up her hand.

Rahul was rooted to the spot. He was gripping the railing for support. In that split second he decided to go upstairs to the roof instead of going after Neha. She didn't want him with her, after all.

The terrace had a completely relaxed scene. People in twos and threes sitting around on the floor, beer and whisky bottles toppled over in the centre, like a glass bonfire. Rahul was sitting and chilling with a couple of others from his batch, leaning against the wall. They had just emptied half a bottle of vodka in shots. Someone gave him a couple of joints where they were sitting. He was in the process of lighting it up when Ritesh walked in.

'Dude!! Welllll...welcome! People, give it up for my man, my army man!' Rahul slurred his words a little.

Ritesh dropped down next to Rahul.

'Woah, man. How much of what has he had?' he asked the group, taking the joint from Rahul and taking a hit for himself.

'Dunno, he's been here a while though.'

'Lost count,' Rahul added.

'Hahaha,' Ritesh laughed. 'You need some food in you, bro! Let's go.'

He helped Rahul get up and pushed him towards the door.

'Mixing drinks man! Rookie mistake. You smell of whiskey and vodka, apart from the smoke. Get in there, wash up,' Ritesh took Rahul into the boy's washroom and pointed at the sink.

Rahul splashed some water on his face and straightened up slowly, 'Good to go, bro.'

Ritesh shook his head and lead him downstairs to the party.

'Did you have a fight with Neha? She looked pissed as hell when she got back.'

Rahul shrugged.

'Sit here,' Ritesh pulled up a chair when they got to the auditorium, and gave him some water to drink. 'I'll get you some food,' Ritesh went to get the food and search for Rehan.

Rahul looked at the dancers in the middle of the hall. *Where is she? Did she leave? Shit.*

He noticed Ritesh standing with Rehan near the buffet, piling some snacks onto a plate. Ten steps from him stood Neha along with Nitin and a few other people, they were moving to the centre of the dance floor. Neha was looking towards the doors often, and this time she must have caught him sitting at the table alone, watching her. Some third year guy whom he knew had been up on the terrace, pulled her into the circle they'd made and was dancing with her, hidden from view. As she stepped out, again, Nitin followed her and said something. She must have not got it because he stepped closer and said in her ear. She stood really close as he bent down to hear her response in his ear. He nodded and walked her to the refreshment area, his hand on her back.

Rahul could bear it no longer. He stood, and threw the glass of water to the side where it bounced off the chair and shattered. It's noise barely registering under the thump of the DJ's music.

He walked towards Neha and Nitin as they were returning with cokes in their hand.

'Neha.'

'Hey, Rahul sir, having a good time?' Nitin asked.

Neha didn't even look up at him. She turned to the side and started walking.

'Neha, I am talking to you,' Rahul reached out and grabbed her shoulder. The sudden jerk made her spill the drink.

'Don't touch me Rahul,' said Neha, shrugging out of his touch.

'Hey, what's the problem?' Nitin came forward and took the glass from Neha and put both his and hers behind them on the table.

Rahul stepped forward again. As Neha backed up, she tripped towards Nitin, who steadied her, asking if she's fine.

He noticed Nitin's hands on her arms and flipped. He grabbed Neha roughly and pulled her to his side, while he swung his other arm to smash his closed fist against Nitin's face.

A few onlookers screamed as Neha stared at Rahul in disbelief. She got her wrist free and rushed towards Nitin who had fallen to the floor, his nose broken and bleeding profusely. Even in his drunken state, Rahul knew how to land a punch. A couple of other drunk third years who got alerted by the screams, charged towards Rahul.

Rahul who couldn't believe Neha went to Nitin stood there defenseless.

Before the boys could raise their fists, Ritesh and Rehan stepped in. Ritesh's reputation was very well-known and drunk or not, no one dared to mess with him.

'Don't even think about it!' Ritesh roared.

The music stopped.

A crowd had collected around them by now. The professors were looking in their direction.

Ritesh growled, 'I do not want any problems here. Rehan, take Rahul back to the hostel, I'll take care of this.'

Rahul kept staring at Neha, who looked shocked with the blood and gore. Rehan tugged at him to get him moving as Ritesh went to help Nitin get up. His final glimpse was of Neha looking at him with disgust; an expression that would haunt him for life.

CHAPTER 13

AIIMS, Delhi

Present Day, 11 October 2011, 8.00 a.m.

'How come you've never spoken about this before?' Rehan asked Rahul as they made their way to the low stone hedges lining the garden in front of the building. They had just got themselves a cup of tea and sandwiches from the stall near the parking lot.

They had sat vigil along with Ritesh's parents all night, and had only stepped out now to stretch their backs a bit. The early morning sun was shining over the multitude of visitors and patients entering the hospital. Visiting hours were about to start and queues were starting to form.

'I dunno. Never really let myself think about it too much. I see her pictures on Facebook from time to time. Kinda hard to deal with. So kept it inside me,' Rahul responded, sipping his tea.

'You should have spoken to her or messaged her at least; explaining your side of the story and listening to hers.'

'These are matters of the heart, Rehan. This is no logical process flow diagram where you put a decision box and say if yes go here, if no go there. It's complicated, but simple too.

I told her how I felt. She too could have gotten in touch with me. She didn't. So there, I lost another person I thought I would have in my life. I had realized that night that she would be the only other woman apart from mom who would have space in my heart. That didn't work out...' Rahul's voice softened.

'Do you still love her?' asked Rehan.

'Perhaps.'

Rehan shook his head. He didn't say anything, but he knew his friend was still such a kid when it came to matters of the heart. He couldn't say anything given that he himself had no experience like this, but as a third person, he could see clearly where Rahul and Neha were standing and why. *If Ritesh knew, he would have knocked some sense into this duffer.*

'Is she why you're in Pune and not Delhi?'

Rahul shrugged at his friend's question.

'And work's fine? What about your project for the US? What's happening with that?'

'Work's okay. The plans are still to be finalized, just finished giving my presentation for the US project. I am hoping for the best.' Rahul crossed his fingers.

'Inshallah, it will be.' Rehan smiled and placed his hands on Rahul's shoulders.

'By the way any idea about Jackal, or should I say Dr Jackal? Where is he?'

'No idea, bro. He's not even on any social media,' Rehan said. 'Wonder what became of him. He was always so mysterious with what he was doing. The only time he opened out was when he was hanging out with us and taking part in our craziness.'

'How's Bhiwadi? Your boss still loves you, you lucky dog?'

'Haha. Bhiwadi is Bhiwadi. Same old. Some new. It's time you took a trip down. Ammi was missing you,' Rehan smiled.

Rahul smiled back at him.

'When was the last time we were in Delhi together? Only right after the final exam? We traced all our favourite routes and haunts. Remember the all-night snacks at Cumsum and then Paranthe Wali Gali in the morning and that bridge we climbed and sat on in old Delhi?'

'Yaa! Paharganj wala café? All those firangs smoking up, remember? Damn. What a chill time we had. We didn't sleep all night, just kept riding around,' Rehan added, nostalgic.

'That was the night after Jackal disappeared right? He'd left a note in my room that he sucked at goodbyes and was just leaving. A**hole. He should have met us once before leaving,' Rahul added now playing around with his lighter. They were both done with their chai.

'You still haven't given up then?' Rehan said, nodding to Rahul's lighter.

'Ahh, man. I try every day. He,' Rahul said nodding his head towards Ritesh, 'told me at least once a week that this habit of mine will kill me before he...dies,' his voice choking with unsaid emotions.

Rehan was looking at the building too. He gripped Rahul's shoulder in support.

'Rehan, can I ask something?'

'Ya, sure.'

'Will Ritesh also leave me like the others?'

Rehan felt his mobile vibrate right then. He checked it as he contemplated his response. An easy one.

'Can I answer you Rahul?'

'Yes.'

'He will not leave us. I got a message from uncle. Ritesh is awake,' Rehan breathed a sigh of relief, 'Let's go.'

Both of them dashed towards the ICU. Their friend was waiting for them.

Mr Dhawan Senior was sitting with his brother-in-law in the ICU waiting room. He looked exhausted, but refused to move to get some rest. The boys walked up to him just as Mrs Dhawan, Ritesh's mother, stepped out through the curtained glass doors that led to the ICU chamber. Rahul and Rehan bent down to touch both their feet, but were caught in hugs before they could complete the traditional greeting they followed with Ritesh's parents.

Mrs Dhawan smiled at them, 'The doctor is with him right now but baba was asking for you. We told him you're here. He's waiting. He said he's tired of lying down and wants to go on a bike ride with you both.'

Rehan and Rahul hugged her and moved towards the ICU.

Ritesh's eyes lit up as he caught sight of his two brothers walking up towards him. The doctor shook his head indulgently as he realized that Major Dhawan had tuned him out the moment he noticed those two boys. *Ritesh Dhawan might be the best the NIA has, a Major and all, but he is still just a 29-year-old boy. Nothing like his best friends to make him feel his age.*

Rehan and Rahul were looking at him anxiously, warily as they saw the doctor and the machines plugged into him. He was covered with white bandages across his ribs, his legs in casts, and a brace around his neck to counter any spinal cord movement while he healed. And all this was just on the outside.

Apparently, his insides were more screwed up than he could count. The exhilaration running through him on seeing his friends was enough. He saw the resolve in their eyes to hide their emotions, he smiled.

'Major, what's this now? We know you said the next time we meet we'll go for a holiday, but you've started early! Already on bed rest, haan?' Rehan said mockingly. He walked to the farther side of the bed and took out the taweez ammi had sent. He lovingly touched Ritesh's forehead, and proceeded to tie the thread around Ritesh's bare arm. Ritesh looked intently at Rehan and blinked. His face was sore with many bruises on it from the fall and the fight, but he managed to give a huge smile, 'Rehan.'

Rehan smiled and sat down next to him, holding onto his fingers. Rahul had in the meantime come up behind Rehan. 'Your herogiri will never die, will it, oh great one?'

'Peter Parker always said, "With great power comes greater responsibility". You know me, I have a superhero complex,' smirked Ritesh.

Rahul leant down to squeeze his arm, 'You look like shit. How do you feel?'

'Ah, on top of the world actually. They have me so drugged up right now, I don't feel a thing,' Ritesh laughed softly.

Rehan looked up at Ritesh and asked him, 'Was it worth it? Worth risking your life like this?

Ritesh smiled, 'I knew you'd ask me that. This isn't the first time I've been hurt in combat. This wasn't the first time I risked my neck for the country. But if you ask me whether it's worth it...I'd say yes. Yes, every time. I see you and Rahul and my family in every person I try to save. And so, I can't look away. I can't walk away. The destination of the path does not define its virtue, my friend. You remember guys, we used to ask every kid in college if they had GMD? And they thought it was a joke. It was not a joke. It was a test of their acceptance of reality. If you have GMD you accept reality and do not pretend to live your life on others' terms. Be it society or anybody else. You have to desire what you want to do, yourself, instead of living as directed by someone else.'

After a moment he continued, 'I followed what I believed in. People seldom do that. They do what is convenient and they repent. I will not. Find what drives you guys. Pune and Bhiwadi might be comfortable, but is it really you? Does it make you feel like anything is achievable? Is it greatness you aspire to? Look for GMD. It's in you. Revel in it. Don't forget...'

Ritesh's voice seemed to break. Rehan asked him if his throat was dry, and he pointed towards some ice chips on the bedside table. He quietly placed a few shards of ice on Ritesh's tongue and Rahul spoke up, 'Now you just shut your mouth and take rest. Nobody can win from you in war of words, or even a war actually.'

Ritesh burst out laughing. His infectious grin making both the boys laugh out too. The ICU warden shushed them with a finger on his lips.

'Bas, now you've got to get better. You're a fighter na? You have to walk out of this ICU on your own two feet.' Rehan said to him.

'Guys...no matter what happens, I will always be a part of you, present in your memories.'

Rahul spoke up, 'Don't be an ass. Nothing is happening except you're going to get better and we're kidnapping you and going for a bike ride to Kasol.'

'Rehan, Rahul,' Ritesh held on to their hands and said in an emotional yet firm voice, 'take care of ma and pa, please... till I can't.'

Both the boys looked back at him expressionless and glistening eyes and saluted.

The clouds roared on top of their voice. Thick water droplets hit the dry parching ground and moments later they were accompanied by millions of other droplets pouring continuously. This was retreat of the monsoon. But it was as if the heavens were crying inconsolably. Their son had left this world. A short journey of life—well lived, well loved. Ritesh's eyes remain closed to the hauntingly beautiful thunderstorm the city woke up to the next morning.

The stormy grey-black sky and howling winds mourned the loss of one of India's true son and brother. Ritesh's family accompanied by Rahul and Rehan and Lt Vikram, who had been here with the family diligently through their days of waiting, were enclosed in the conference room.

Mrs Dhawan had finally lost her will to stay strong. She was being held up by an inconsolable Mr Dhawan. The splitting image of his son, he was the age Ritesh would never reach. Rehan wept with short wracking sobs, looking into his hands. Rahul wondered if his friend was praying or just watching the tears collect in his palms. He, on the other hand, couldn't stop staring at Ritesh's father. He remembered a conversation he'd had with Ritesh one drunken night, about growing old and grey. Something to do with smoking and dying. The one time Rahul responded to Ritesh's thoughts about mortality. *You're going to die before me if you don't quit that.*

Dude. My brother. You always say that. I'll stop one day. I will. We will grow old men together. Rehan will lose his hair, I will be a hippy...no...you will be a hippie with your long hair and I'll just...

And, we'll come back here to this rooftop at MSU and take pictures, smoke up and do the race again. I'll still beat your ass, you know, you'll be huffing and puffing with your cigarettes.

No, I won't. But I might have a receding hairline, no thanks to my dad. I hope I don't look like him when I grow up. But you're lucky. You are just like uncle.

Yeah. When I see him, it's like looking at myself in the mirror, only twenty years down the line. Ma says she has the best of both worlds...

Rahul's eyes were stinging. He turned to look outside the window. He felt unsettled. The storm raged outside but inside the room there was an unnerving quietness. As he stared into nothingness, tears fell from his eyes. He blinked them away, his eyes focused on the reflection in the window. The incandescent lighting of the room was projecting a figure so familiar, Rahul's breath caught in his throat. He would never see his friend again, his brother. Or grow old with him. Or see him as clearly as he sees Mr Dhawan Senior. He shut his eyes to the likeness and the storm, wishing he were out in the rain, on a distant rooftop smoking with his friend or screaming with the agony his heart was in.

A military band was playing when the cavalcade of cars entered Brar Square Crematorium in Delhi Cantt the next morning. Rahul and Rehan had spent the previous evening conversing with the officers from Ritesh's NIA team and their

Director. Ritesh would be offered the full 21 gun salutation and be cremated with full state honours.

They noticed through their car window the crowd that had assembled at the venue. A lot of people in uniforms, civilians too and a few media vans. Ritesh had made the news.

Mr and Mrs Dhawan were escorted by the Director of the NIA to the makeshift tents that had been put up for the occasion. The rest of the family followed—Ritesh's aunts, uncles and cousins. Rahul and Rehan stood at the rear end of the procession. They waited in line as the hearse doors opened and Ritesh's body was carried out on a wooden palette, heaved onto the shoulders of Ritesh's team—Lieutenants Vikram and Rashid and others they had not met. The men in uniform were drenched in water pouring from the heavens. With the coffin resting on their shoulders, they marched ahead making a cacophony from their heavy military boots splashing water from the poodles of water that had accumulated in the ground.

Rahul and Rehan made their way to Ritesh's parents' side. Rehan held on to Dhawan uncle, a father figure to him since he lost his own. He was standing stoic. His red eyes, the only indication of emotion. Rahul put his arm around Ritesh's mom, supporting her, as she cried copiously and seemed to sway every few minutes.

The state followed their customs, as the family watched hordes of seniors and juniors salute their son, their brother and place wreaths of flowers at his feet. The Commander of Ritesh's Army unit and the Director of the NIA both came forward to present the Indian Flag that had been covering Ritesh's body to his parents.

Ritesh's body was then transferred to the pyre. The guard of honour stood by the side, with their rifles at the ready. A pandit signalled to the family to come forward to light the pyre. It was at this point that both Mrs and Mr Dhawan seemed to lose their hold on their emotions. Ritesh's mother let out a wail that went unheard under the music of the band, her sister and nieces stepped forward to hold on to her while Rehan moved to stand with Mr Dhawan. Ritesh's father's hands shook, and for the first time since Rehan and Rahul had known him, he seemed like a frail old man. Losing his son seemed to have aged him incredibly. They both supported him as they walked towards the pyre. The rain stopped and gave way to the ceremony to proceed. The pandit stepped forward to hand Mr Dhawan the lit log of wood, with which he would need to light the rest, but he couldn't extend his hands forward. Rehan and Rahul both looked at each other and bent low to touch his feet. As they came forward, Rahul said to Dhawan uncle, 'We are your sons too. We are here for you.'

Ritesh's dad looked touched as he wept uncontrollably. Rehan took the log from the pandit and held it towards Dhawan uncle and Rahul. All three of them, circled the pyre twice, as instructed by the pandit and lit it up, as the salutations from the guns went off. The three stood there, motionless, stupefied by the act they just performed. It seemed so final. A young, bright energy that was Ritesh's soul was now no longer theirs. They would never see him again, hold on to him, laugh or cry with him. No longer would he smile at them. Lt Vikram was close by; he tugged at the three of them, to bring them a safe distance away from the pyre. The pandit had started chanting shloks, while the fire danced merrily around the wood.

Ritesh's father hugged Rehan, holding him close like he would never hold his son again. Ritesh had given them two more sons, his adopted brothers as he left them, but nothing would dull the pain of Ritesh's absence and the longing of his presence.

Rahul, his vision blurry with tears, looked up at the sky. The clouds were rolling in, playing hide and seek with a pale sun. His eyes caught a horde of news reporters taking note of the proceedings, and cameramen angling for a good shot at Ritesh's parents and the family. He shook his head; vultures. The media needed to stop focusing on the agony that aunty and uncle were going through. He looked away. He went and stood with Rehan to one side, as guests paid their condolences to the family while exiting the crematorium, Rahul looked over at the civilians. Foremost among them, a well-dressed familiar lady caught his attention. Professor Lalita Verma, Miss Lilli, her eyes shielded by sunglasses, wearing her white trademark sari was holding a handkerchief to her face. She too had noticed him, she nodded at them and smiled softly. Behind her a few paces, were more people he recognized. Pankaj Bhoj, or a larger, heftier version of him, stood with PSO's behind him. He might be a well-known politician now, but Rahul knew he had kept in touch with Ritesh over the years. Himanshu was here with Nazia, they must have come in from Bareilly, he thought. He knew they both worked and lived there as a happily married couple now. Behind them, he recalled vague faces, people from college, their juniors, even a few seniors, a few more professors, their college director. He could make out a few people from Ritesh's school whom he had met over the years.

Rehan too was overwhelmed by the number of people that had shown up to see Ritesh off. He looked across at the hordes of people affected by Ritesh's death—civilians and defence personnel alike. He was proud of his brother, a single soul that had touched so many lives, made a difference.

Rakesh baba, Rahul's man friday had been trying to catch their attention. Rehan noticed him towards the back and signalled his namaste. He pulled Rahul out of his reverie and pointed towards the gates. Rahul's father, Mr Bhatia had come for the funeral. Rahul looked at him stunned. This was a level of involvement Rahul did not expect from his father. Rakesh baba kept gesturing for Rahul to join them and as he took a shaky step forward, he jerked to a stop.

Wearing a white linen suit and a yellow dupatta, Rahul saw a face he thought he once knew, he once thought he loved. She too seemed to have noticed his stare, as she stilled amongst the moving crowd. Neha Khare, had come forward after half a decade.

CHAPTER 14

Lost Lake, Mangar Village, Aravalli Hills
Gurgaon-Faridabad Border

Later That Day

They pedalled hard up the stony pathways, hoping the exertion would empty their minds and allow them some peace. Both of them couldn't bear to go to the flat at Safdarjung today. Lt Vikram had offered to pack up Ritesh's belongings and have it delivered to Amritsar, a task they assured him they will do in the next couple of days. Ritesh had given copy of his house keys to Lt Vikram. Not that he had been there much—he'd always been on some mission or the other, but having a place to call his own had been important to Ritesh. It had also been closer to HQ; dedicated that he was to his job, he wanted to be closer. His parent's too had not minded, supporting their son's desires.

Today, after the excruciating process of committing the final act of letting their brother go, Rahul and Rehan just needed to escape, they needed to process the fact that their trio, would now, never be called that again. That they would never be refereed again, that they were down from three R's to two. They needed to mourn, in private. Being with Ritesh's family had made them hold back, be strong for them, fulfil duties that fell upon their shoulders. But this time, right now, what they needed was to be able to shout out into the night, to vent out their building desolation.

Driving back home that afternoon after ensuring that Ritesh's parents were settled at their relative's place, the boys had left for home. Just driving aimlessly for a while since they both didn't feel like going home. Rahul, didn't feel like meeting his father. He couldn't understand why he had shown up at the funeral. What was he trying to prove? And Rehan, well Rehan needed to scream. The proper, posh Jor Bagh mansion might not be the right space for it.

'Let's go to Mangar hilltop?' Rehan said in the quiet car.

Rahul looked at Rehan gratefully and switched directions; heading now towards the Gurgaon-Faridabad highway.

They stopped to borrow bikes from the Pedal-Up Studio in Gurgaon. It was a cycle shop owned by Vikas Gupta, an avid cyclist himself whom the trio had befriended during their rides to the trails.

'How are you guys holding up? I saw Ritesh's news on TV. Very sad. Very sad. He was such a good soul. God bless you both.' Vikas said.

Rehan and Rahul both nodded and thanked him. He reminded them to handover the bikes to the guard as they left, since he would be off in another couple of hours.

—⚋—

Of the many developments that this hidden oasis had seen over the past few years, adventure camps and encroachers setting up shop in the area, they were really pleased to find that their hidden spot and Mangar baba's tiny hut had remained largely untouched. They trekked up the last few dozen metres of their trail, carrying their bikes up. The gulmohar tree, still stood unchanged, tall and majestic. It was a relief to exert themselves to get to the top. Being exhausted felt like a better emotion than the internal agony they were both in.

Mangar baba, who proffered them his sage advice from time to time, brought them chai, keen on maintaining custom.

'Where is Ritesh baba?' He asked, surprised to see two, instead of three.

Rahul looked at Mangar baba with red eyes and signalled towards the sky. The old man looked at both of them and understood why they brought such repressed energies with them today.

'You are sad. But do you realize why?'

'Because...because he's left us. Because we won't get to see him again. Because we won't be able to talk to him, ever again. It hurts,' Rahul cried out, his emotions swelling to a tipping point, as he brushed his eyes roughly.

Baba looked at him calmly, lit up his joint and sat on the boulder facing the lake. 'Beta, life is nothing but a game of gaining and losing. The problem with mankind is that we take it personally. We become possessive about those with us. It is the loss we miss. And you notice, it is all about you? Not about the person who's gone. "You" won't see him again. "You" won't talk to him again...when did it become about you and not him? It is our physical attachment, our possessiveness that makes us unhappy. Yes, his body is no longer there for you to see, but his spirit, his soul, his ideas, his beliefs, his thoughts remain with you. He has given you a bit of himself over the years, hasn't he?' He looked out at the lake. The sun was making its slow trudge down into the horizon. Further up in sky an eagle circled and made a loud call while returning to her nest. Rahul was staring down at the ground, tears streaking down his face. Rehan, looked at Mangar baba silently, trying to draw strength from his words.

'People are brought into your life for a reason. Maybe your friend did what he came to do. He fulfilled his life's mission. You should be celebrating his life. Celebrate that he existed, for however short a period. The sun comes up every day, and disappears at a set time. Its existence is not validated by us. It does what it has to. It comes up because we need light and energy. The universe has ordained that it rises and falls every day. Look at you two. Sitting here and missing the beauty of the sunset. The sun is offering you a moment in time. A moment, which will be beautiful to you. Everything is to be celebrated, even if it doesn't make sense to you right now. It will later. It is fulfilling its destiny...' Baba paused to relight his joint. He took a deep drag and looked at both the boys and then towards the lake again, 'Didn't he always want to save people, do something good for humankind, for his nation, your friend? Did he do it? Was he successful? Did he teach you something? If you miss him, remember him. Remember the good. Let it fill you up with energy. Everyone who dies, leaves a bit of themselves with those they loved. You three, are brothers, friends; each other's companions. Has he not left part of his soul in you? Aren't you different because of him? Yes, it is human nature to hurt, human nature to feel pain and to miss, but it is also inherently a human trait to heal.'

He looked at Rehan and Rahul, both crying freely now, their breathing sporadic, hands shaking and with their bodies quivering with the sobs wracking them.

'You will heal,' he finished and let them be as he walked back into his hut.

28, Jor Bagh, New Delhi

The boys had made it back to Rahul's place in the wee hours of the morning. After getting out of Mangar forest, they had continued driving around, both evaluating what Mangar baba had said, lost in their thoughts about Ritesh's impact on their lives. They were recalling instances from their lives, small moments that seemed momentous now; everyday jokes and laughter that now formed an intricate part of their history with Ritesh. Rahul stopped the car at one of the roadside thekas on the old Gurgaon-Faridabad road to pick up some liquid courage, to deal with a future without their brother in it. They started off with toasts to Ritesh's memory and steadily progressed to using alcohol to forget the past few days.

At 3 a.m. that morning Rakesh baba and Rajinder bhaiya, the guard, ran outside the house to support Rahul and Rehan and help them to their respective bedrooms. Both of the boys, unsteady on their feet and with blurry eyes, failed to notice Rajesh Bhatia, in his dressing gown, watching them stumble into the house from his private balcony.

—∞—

Being intoxicated had finally afforded Rahul and Rehan a few hours' sleep. They woke up in the morning to headache medicines and freshly squeezed orange juice. Rakesh baba had woken them both up and got them ready for they had to go with Ritesh's family to the cremation ground one last time, to pick up Ritesh's ashes.

On their way back from Ritesh's masi's house, Rahul received a phone call from his office. He couldn't believe that the world was carrying on living like nothing had changed, while from where he sat, both his and Rehan's lives had changed drastically and even though both the boys had dealt with loss of parents before, this time, it felt deeper, for Ritesh had been family they had chosen.

'Yes...oh.' and after a pause, 'Thank you. Yes, I'll check my email and get back to you later today.'

Rehan looked at Rahul curiously, 'What's up?'

'That US project I was telling you about? I got it. They want me to report on Monday and finalize all the details with the office. They're setting up a special meeting with the consulate officer for the visa next week. They want me to go within this month. Their local office will make all the arrangements for my stay.'

Rehan looked at Rahul's stunned expression and smiled, 'Congratulations bhai. Your dreams are coming true.'

Rahul smiled back at him casually.

They drove the remainder of the ride in silence, both immersed in their own thoughts.

Rehan was thinking about Bhiwadi. Rahul's news about the US was keenly similar to a dream he had had once. He remembered his father's last wish and wondered if he had followed his heart, would things be different. Can not the heart's desires also change over time? What kept him in Bhiwadi all these years? He continued giving his sweat and blood to the city his father believed in, and he did so, dedicatedly and sincerely. But, was it enough? When Ritesh asked us about GMD, is this what he meant? Five years ago,

Rehan changed the course of his life to follow what his heart told him was right at that time, to understand his father's point of view and fulfil his vision, and now the very same heart was questioning if it was enough.

Rahul couldn't believe his luck, here was his dream, being handed to him on a silver platter; a chance to step out from his father's influence once and for all and make something of himself, in a faraway land, leaving behind every memory and every person from his current life. He vowed to stay connected to Rehan, his one positive possession from life. He was thrilled that he had a chance to leave behind the pain from the last few days, and the mess that his life was—with his father confusing him by coming to Ritesh's funeral and Neha popping back in front of him. He hadn't confronted either of them and wasn't planning to. It would be easier to just get away from it all.

When they got home, Rahul informed Rakesh baba that they would both be heading out later that day. Rahul flying back to Pune and Rehan to Bhiwadi, leaving Ritesh's family to immerse his ashes as they deemed fit. Life was to continue as it was.

A little while later, Rehan came down to get himself some tea when he saw Rakesh baba talking to a very well dressed lady sitting in the lounge. He looked up at Rehan and quickly introduced them.

'Sunanda madam, this is Rehan baba. He's Rahul baba's best friend.'

Rehan hurried forward, his hands folded in a namaste and later extended out in a handshake as he took the palm Sunanda Arora offered. 'Rehan, pleasure meeting you. I have heard about you before, but it is good to finally place you. I am Sunanda Arora, Rahul's masi.'

'Thank you, aunty. I, didn't know you ah...'

'Existed? Not surprising. I shifted to Paris a few months before Rahul's mother passed away. Most unfortunate. Maybe if I had been here, things might have been different. I very rarely come down to Delhi though. Anyway,' she said, brushing her shoulder-length hair back, 'do you know where he is? Rahul? Is he sleeping?'

Rehan shrugged, 'I don't know. I just packed and came downstairs directly.'

'Don't worry, Rehan baba. I will go see if Rahul baba is awake. I will call him downstairs. I have told the cook to bring you some tea and refreshments.' Rakesh baba went upstairs to check.

Sunanda beckoned Rehan to be seated, 'Come, tell me more about you while we wait for Rahul.'

—∞—

A short while later Rahul bounded down the stairs. Although it was years since they last met, his masi was the closest thing he had to his mother. Elder than his mom by a few years, she had very little resemblance to her but he had some fond memories of playing with her while sitting on his mother's lap during festivals. So far, they had Skyped a few times and spoke to each other on birthdays, but seeing her in the flesh after so many years suddenly brought to the fore the feeling of familial ties. He went straight up to her and gave her a bear hug as she got up. Apart from Rehan's ammi's hugs, this was the closest he had felt to a mother's embrace.

He stepped back after a long while, refusing to let go of her, and exclaimed, 'Look at you masi! You look amazing. You haven't aged a day since I was a kid.'

'Rehan, masi is mumma's elder sister. Uncle is a diplomat with the foreign embassy in Paris.'

'Rahul, he's the High Commissioner now,' she said smiling indulgenty.

'Oh sorry. How is he? Is he also here? How come you're here? Where are Sahil and Shanaia?' Rahul looked around the room as if expecting to see them pop up from behind a sofa.

'Everyone's well. It's just me this time…' she patted Rahul's hand, held in her own.

'Let me see you properly. You have grown so much. I'm sorry, I missed most of your growing up years. I wanted to call you to me, to have you finish your schooling and do your college with me, but Rajesh bhai saab…' she left off.

'Yeah. I can imagine,' replied Rahul with a look of disdain. 'Why would the great Rajesh Bhatia ever want something good for his son?'

'No Rahul…'

'No masi, you don't know. Anyway, have something to eat. Here.' Rahul said gesturing towards the coffee table laden with tea time savouries.

'Why don't you stay another day Rehan? Do you need to go back today itself?' Sunanda looked at Rehan.

'Well, aunty…'

'But, masi, I'm also going today evening. I have a late night flight back to Pune. So, we'll both be leaving together. I'll drop him to the station before heading to the airport.'

'Oh, Rahul. I must insist. Stay back one more day, please. For me. Both of you. Go tomorrow.'

Rehan left them to it. He went upstairs to call ammi and Mr Chaudhary and let them know of his changed plans. He went back to the room that he and Ritesh used to share, whenever they stayed at Rahul's place during college. As he finished his calls, he saw Sunanda aunty and Rahul strolling through the gardens in the dusk. He felt happy for his friend. Distant or not, Rahul needed a mother's touch, now more than ever.

He went and lay back down on the bed, his thoughts keeping him busy. He felt the same hollowness he had gone through when abba passed away six years ago. No matter how hard he tried, the tears wouldn't come anymore. He surmised, he spent all of them at Mangar baba's yesterday. His thoughts fast forwarded to Rahul's news. He too would be leaving him. Sure, the manner of distance would be different, but nevertheless, he was about to lose another one of his closest friends.

Rahul and Sunanda masi walked in slow circles around the circumference of the garden.

'So, where is Mr Rajesh Bhatia? How come he isn't here to welcome you? Does he know you're here?' Rahul asked spitefully.

Sunanda patted the arm she was holding on to and said, 'Rahul...there are some things you should know...'

CHAPTER 15

—⋘—

Rahul was smashing his fists against the punching bag hanging from the trolley chain in the ceiling of his gym room at home. His muscular upper body naked till torso was drenched in sweat. Rehan found him there, punching his heart out.

He went and shut the music playing blaringly loud.

'Rahul, what's the matter?'

Rahul held on to the punching bag with both his hands as Rehan walked up to him.

'Bro?'

Rahul's red eyes were the only indication he had been crying, and that all the sweat on his face wasn't just that. He looked up at Rehan and said, 'I can't take it anymore yaar! I...I can't deal with anything anymore.'

Rehan gave him the bottle of water he had picked up from the table, 'Drink up.'

'Tell me what happened? Did Rajesh uncle say something?'

'Papa...'

Over the next half hour Rahul recalled and relayed to Rehan his conversation with Sunanda masi.

—⋘—

'Rahul...there are some things you should know...'

'Like what masi?'

'About your father'

'I don't want to talk about him.'

'This time, Rahul, you will listen. You don't have to talk. There are things you should know about your mom. I am surprised your Dad didn't tell you in all the years since her death. That was, is, very gracious of him. Even in death he has preserved her memory for you. And, that's more than I could have asked from him.'

'What are you talking about masi?'

'Let's sit, Rahul.' She pointed at the lone bench nestled near a small fountain in their garden lawn.

'You were what...just over eight-years-old when the strains of your dad's hard work started catching up with your mom. My sister, always pampered, always adored, couldn't deal with coming second to her husband's work.' She raised her hand to stop Rahul interrupting her. 'When she married your father, and she desperately wanted to...we took the rishta to your dadaji. She was infatuated with his good looks and his money and the lifestyle he could offer her. He was the only son, he used to work with his dad back then. Your dadaji's age was catching up to him. No matter how hard he tried, he just couldn't give the company as many hours as were required. So your dad had to pick up the slack. He didn't mind it. But, now he had his young wife and new son too. And for a while it worked well. Your mom, who had chosen your dad, knowing how busy he is, he was like this before you came along. For 11 years of their marriage, eight of which were with you, your mom supported your dad through his success and hardships, as he did both his work and his dad's. The economy was running downhill, like you wouldn't believe. By 1991, your dad was running flat out against the economic slump, and yet providing the same luxurious lifestyle that you and your mom were used to by then.'

'Your dad used to travel to Europe and Asia a lot for his work. Back when you were a toddler, she used to leave you with us or sometimes take you along as she accompanied your father on his business trips. These trips lasted days, sometimes weeks. After a while, she became socially involved with her kitty parties and her socialite friends, and you were also going to school. So travelling became secondary for her. She was happy with her circle of friends and you. The discord started when she began pressurizing Rajesh to stop those trips, to stop working so hard. And mind you, this is during peak recession in India. Anjali's life was one quick downward spiral. In a matter of seven months, life changed so drastically, that no one could do anything about it. She started spending more time with her so called friends—wives of other rich and influential men. They were a depressed lot. Always bitching, pardon my language, about something or the other. Drinking, playing cards, smoking, shopping. That's all their lives were about. Your mother too started changing. She was drinking more, started staying unhappy. She became whiny, clingy. And then the fights started. Your dad couldn't understand at that time what changed. He tried getting her involved in the business, but she didn't want that. He told her to change her friends, and well, you can imagine how that turned out. He made her see a psychiatrist. He used to call me for advice, used to remind me to check up on her and you every time he went off on a trip.'

'Oh but she loved you. No doubt. But even all her love for you wasn't enough, maybe. She needed attention. She was always like that; always the person who loved being pampered. Rajesh continued pampering her. Showering her with gifts and diamonds, whatever she asked for. But she wanted all this and more. She wanted attention, being flirted with, being taken out for dinner and lunches. She wanted to show off her husband to her group of friends, but alas, was mostly alone...sometime in the last three months of her life, she met someone...you remember Yograj uncle?'

Rahul, who was listening to his masi with rapt attention, swallowed hard and nodded, 'The one in Abu Dhabi? Dad's business partner?' He couldn't fathom this part of his mother's life. He didn't remember any of it.

Sunanda scoffed, 'Yes. His business partner. He knew Rajesh since his college days. And had at that time recently come back from Abu Dhabi. He wanted to start a new business or something at that time. He was out of funds. Your dad used some of his contacts to get things going for Yograj. He used to dine with your family a lot those days. Everyone became very close. Rajesh treated Yograj like a brother, and welcomed him to their home whenever he was in town. What happened was that your mother became close to him too. Well, who can blame her right? Yograj wasn't travelling. He was always around whenever Anjali needed something done. He escorted her to her friend's parties or lunches at times. Slowly he became the shoulder she was crying on; crying about her fate, about how lonely she is and about how her husband doesn't care for her.'

'It was your birthday party. Rajesh had been in England sorting out a crisis. He was supposed to reach in the evening for your party, before you cut the cake. But somehow, he got delayed. I think he came by the next flight. But over here,

Anjali just lost it. She had been drinking since morning; you remember, I helped you cut your cake then? I'd told you mumma was feeling sick? I didn't let her come downstairs that evening because she was so drunk.'

Rahul couldn't believe what he was hearing. He just stared at his masi, his hands shaking and his throat getting dry. He didn't know if he wanted to hear anymore, but she continued. 'I think it happened when the party was going on. Yograj went upstairs to check on your mother. In the meantime, your father reached home. He was with us for a while and then as the guests started leaving, he went upstairs too, to check on Anjali too.

'That was the only day I saw Rajesh lose control. He stormed out of the house. Your friends and guests had gone by then. It was just us, family. Yograj and Anjali stumbled out after him. Disheveled, messy looks about them. It was then that I knew what Anjali had done; what Yograj and Anjali did to your father.

'Rajesh stayed at my house that night. There was a huge scene. When he had come back here, Anjali was sitting in the living room, waiting for him. As soon as he walked in, she fell to her knees and apologized and begged for forgiveness. Your uncle and I were shocked. You and your cousins were too young to understand, of course. Rajesh picked you up and was taking you with him when she screamed about not separating you from her along with all her regrets and her one time indiscretion with Yograj. But that night, something broke in Rajesh. He had trusted and loved your mother immensely. But, he was looking at your mother like he didn't recognize her. That was the only day I ever knew Rajesh to be furious. He told her, that he wanted to divorce her, but wouldn't because of the boy in his arms. He didn't say anything else, just quietly took you and left. Your uncle went after him to make sure you were both okay.'

'I stayed back to help sort things out with Anjali. But she was gone. She knew too, that all of this was inevitable. Instead of trying to get better, she picked up a bottle and drank herself away. She tried being sober when Rajesh was in town, but he couldn't bear to be in the same room as her. He only came home to see you from time to time and spent nights in your room, after you were asleep. He found solace in his work. Leaving before the sun had risen and coming back much later than dinner time.'

'Now this was the time that your uncle got posted to Paris, and he needed to take me along for all the diplomatic formalities. I took Anjali with me for a few days. Just to distract her. You remember, Rahul? We took you to the Eiffel Tower and on a boat ride? Anjali spent three glorious days, sober and like her usual self, attached to you, like she was breathing you in. She cleared her head out and wrote a letter to Rajesh, explaining everything and all that she felt and was going through. You were both supposed to stay for longer but she insisted on going back.'

'Apparently, you were both fine till she got home. When she walked into her house, her bedroom, she saw Rajesh had moved his things out from there and to the guest bedroom. That's when it hit her that she had lost her husband. From what I understand, the servants told me, that she kept screaming that she's sorry. Rakesh kept taking you out of the house whenever your mom was in a mood like that. She drank from morning to night, every day. Two months later, she overdosed on her whiskey. Rakesh found her in her room, her heart rate very slow. When they got to the hospital, they realized she had had a heart attack and that it couldn't take the strain anymore.'

Wiping the tears off her face, Sunanda continued, 'By the time we got to know and were able to come back, your mother had passed away. Your father, who had been in Bombay, flew back as soon as they took her to the hospital, but she closed her eyes before he got there.'

'No one knew about her affair, no one knew that it was guilt that killed her. Your father to this day hasn't told anyone. Not even you... And I'm surprised, because he could have healed his relationship with you long ago. I guess he didn't want to ruin your mom's memories.'

She put her hand on Rahul head. He was bent over, his head close to his knees, his hands clutching his hair.

'I'm sorry, but you needed to know beta. My intention wasn't to spoil your mother's memories for you, but you are grown up enough to understand, now. What happened with Anjali wasn't your dad's fault, not completely. I'm sorry I didn't come earlier or tell you earlier. Your father doesn't know I've told you. He forbade me from telling you actually, when he called me day before yesterday. He was in anguish over your friend dying. He called me in a panic in the middle of the night in Paris, and said he's booked the tickets, and that I need to be here, for you. Because...because he realized you needed family around you, and I told you all this because I agree with him. You need your family with you Rahul. And your family, your strongest supporter, your father, is right here. And you should know, that whatever happens and wherever you are, your dad is always going to put you first, like he always has—your silent watchful guardian.'

Tears were running down Rehan's face too, by the time Rahul finished. He hugged his friend tight, words bypassing them.

'What are you going to do?'

'I need to see him.'

—⚬—

All the lights were blazing in the house when Rajesh walked in that night. It had been another gruelling day, and his stamina wasn't what it used to be at one point. Rakesh had informed him that Sunanda di had come over today, he wondered if she was staying over for dinner. *Weren't Rahul and Rehan supposed to leave today evening? What's going on?* Rajesh walked into his study to get a glass of single malt before dinner to unwind a bit. But the sight that awaited him left him stupefied in the doorway.

His son was waiting for him in his study, holding two tumblers of what looked like whiskey, with a large balloon that said, 'I'm sorry Papa.' Also in the room were Sunanda and Rehan, both smiling and crying at the same time.

Rahul placed the crystal on the table behind him and walked forward with such a powerful force that he left Rajesh breathless with the massive hug his son had given him. He felt Rahul's arms around him and heard him cry, 'I'm sorry papa, I'm sorry,' over and over again, interspersed with 'I love you papa.' Rajesh dropped his coat and tie as he hugged his son back, tears escaping his eyes too, as he held on to Rahul. His son had finally returned to him.

CHAPTER 16

Aundh, Pune

After dropping Rehan off at the railway station early next morning, Rahul had taken a quick flight back to Pune. The offices were closed today, being a weekend, but first thing on Monday, he knew what he needed to do. He picked up his iPhone and dialled Deepak Agnihotri, his project manager's number.

28, Jor Bagh, Delhi

The sprawling bungalow constructed in neo-classical architecture had never been brighter. The atmosphere inside the house had changed drastically over the weekend. All the staff at the house felt the change and credited it to Bhatia Senior and Junior patching up.

Rajesh Bhatia couldn't remember feeling this light in decades. It was as if he was suffused with new energy. For the first time in a long time, it felt like he could breathe again. Even though Rahul had gone back to Pune, he knew his son was at least close to him at heart. It was more than he could have asked for, this camaraderie with his son. He had let go of the idea of having Rahul join the company nearly five years ago, when they had had a major argument about it, but who knew, there was always hope; life just proved it. Rajesh was wondering how to go about broaching the topic with Rahul when he came over next.

Later that week, when he got home, he debated asking for dinner to be served in his room. He was exhausted, ensuring everything was set up for the trip to Johannesburg later that week. The next few days would be fraught with negotiations with a Chinese firm that were angel investors in the company they were going to be acquiring.

Rakesh, his man Friday, came into his room, all smiles, informing him dinner was ready.

Rakesh, bring me a tray here. I have a lot of work to do, I'll...'

'Saab, you should come downstairs though.' Rakesh interrupted, still smiling. 'Rahul baba is waiting for you for dinner.'

Rajesh's heart leapt. 'I'll be downstairs in a minute.'

'How did your office take the news?'

'Well,' Rahul replied, 'they were a bit disappointed. My boss liked me, so he was keen on me managing the project. But they'll get over the loss.'

'But, you've resigned?'

'Yep.'

'What about your notice period?'

'They waived it off. Didn't want me around after I refused the America project. Also, I only joined the firm six months ago, just a few days short. So it was easily managed, I was still under the probation period.'

'Oh. Okay. Have you thought what you're going to do now?' curious about what Rahul had been thinking of.

'Well, yes. I'm going to negotiate for a job I was born to do,' Rahul said with a cheeky smirk.

'Oh, yes? What would your negotiations entail?'

'I'm a simple man. I'll take weekends off to start with and a jump from my previous salary.'

Rajesh smiled behind his glass of wine. Rakesh had outdone himself with today's dinner.

'What do you feel about travelling?' Rajesh asked, with a straight face. *Two can play this game my son. We are the same blood, after all.*

'I'm going to South Africa day after tomorrow. Would you like to come along? It's a new account. For a new beginning?' he raised his glass inquiringly.

Rahul looked at Rajesh smugly. *Don't miss a chance do you, Dad?*

Rahul too lifted his glass of wine and clinked it with his dad's, toasting a journey towards the future they would embark on together.

Carlton Centre
Prichard Street, Johannesburg, South Africa

For thirty-eight years now, the Carlton Centre stood as a landmark in South Africa. It boasted the prestige of being the tallest building in the country, serving as a tourist attraction and comprising shops in the mall below and offices scattered in the remaining section.

Rahul dressed in a crisp business suit, his short hair gelled and neatly cut in spikes stood watching the city from the 47 floor conference room. The floor-to-ceiling windows made the view truly mesmerizing. They were early. The M&A team, risk management guys, the lawyers, accountants and company secretary from Bhatia Steel made an impressive sight. His dad was busy talking on the phone. Rahul nodded at his dad's assistant and informed her he was stepping out for a smoke.

The small semi-circular enclosure, semi-hidden near the elevator shaft was also encased in glass. It had a window to let out the smoke, but was more like a covered balcony. *Stopping pissed off professionals from jumping to their deaths I suppose* he thought with a grin.

He turned around to see a delegation of Chinese people walk past the corridor towards the conference room.

As he stubbed out the remaining cigarette, he looked up to see a familiar outline—a stocky, bald guy wearing a shining pair of black Greenwich buckle and Louis Vuitton shoes. The golden stripped dark blue tuxedo was a perfect fit. Not an inch more not an inch less. The Bulgaria frameless oval glasses rested in peace on the sharp-pointed nose. With a distinctive walk and hunch he was walking towards the boardroom through which the rest of the delegation had disappeared.

Rahul stumbled out into the corridor and shouted, 'Is that really you, f****r?'

Jai Kishan Amre turned around with a start. He couldn't believe it. The voice calling out to him was one he would never forget. He dropped the files in his hands as he stared at Rahul strutting towards him.

'Holy shit!'

'F**k! It is you! Doctor Jackal! How're you doing man?' Rahul went up to Jackal and half lifted him up in a bear hug.

As he put him down, Jackal hugged Rahul back sheepishly, looking up at him in wondrous curiosity. 'I'm well. How are you? What are you doing here? Aren't you supposed to be in Pune?'

'Wait, how do you know about Pune? We don't know anything about you. You disappeared man. What the hell? And what are you doing here?' Rahul asked, pointing towards first Jackal and then the conference room.

'I have my ways. I'm always updated on people I care about. Oh, and I'm late for a meeting. I'm with those Chinese chaps. We're negotiating a merger with the Bhatia's for my tech...' he trailed off.

Rahul was grinning now, pointing to himself.

Jackal slapped his head with his disfigured hand and exclaimed, 'You're the Bhatia of Bhatia Steel. Damn! How could I miss that?' He laughed out loud.

It was now Rahul's turn to look at Jackal incredulously.

'Wait... Are you the JKA in all those legal documents we had to look over? We thought it must be one of them Chinese guys...' he trailed off. 'You're the one with the patents?'

Jackal was sniggering, 'Yeah, that's me.'

'So you're the guy giving the go ahead, basically?'

'Yeah. They've left it on me. Haha. Let's go show these Chinese people who's the boss.'

Both Rahul and Jackal walked in somberly, each to his own side of the table and with straight faces, got the meeting started. Rajesh Bhatia started off by introducing Rahul to their South African counterparts and the Chinese delegation. He shook hands with the African Board members, now part of Bhatia Steel and bowed his shoulders to the Chinese in their traditional method of greeting.

Rajesh could see the surprise and appreciation in the eyes of the Chinese. He was pleased. 'Good afternoon, ladies and gentlemen.' Rahul said, in Chinese Mandarin, astounding everyone at the table.

'I look forward to working with you in this new venture. I trust you will not mind my attempt at your language,' he continued in English, although he could see that he was successful in his efforts.

He winked at his father from the corner of his eye. His father smiled at him in response.

The other team then gave a brief introduction to Jackal and went ahead with the negotiations on price—the only part that was left to be finalized in this merger and acquisition.

The Bhatia's waited while the Chinese discussed among themselves, the price of giving up their shares and the offer made by them, weighing the pros and cons.

Rahul stood. His dad looked at him questioningly and pointed back at his seat. Rahul nodded at him to wait.

'Our offer to buy your shares is not only reasonable, but as my team and yours will tell you, it is more than what you will get in the market from now till the next five years. The scope of this deal beyond that is vague since we don't know what new government clauses and or policies will be implemented by either of our two countries with regards bilateral trade and direct investments. You are trying to place a value to the technology you bring to the table now, as are we. While you're hoping for the hypothetical, our analysts have worked out real time the costs and ROIs it will bring us. Yes, we are at an upper hand, and I will be honest with you about it simply because we know as well as you do that this technology if not adapted now, and in our industry, it will become redundant against what your competitors are talking of producing two years down the line. Everyone sitting here also knows that the methodology of using this tech is patented by Bhatia Steel. No other competitor in the steel industry will come to you with the offer we have, for precisely this reason, apart from the following; one, they are not close enough to our production power to warrant the tech you offer; two, if the news gets out that we didn't like or use your tech, no other company or industry will want it; three, well... Is there really a reason for me to go on?'

'Mr Nandy,' Rahul said, looking at the company secretary, 'could you please pass the patent papers and the agreement over to Mr Amre, so that he too can have a look at what we offer, to him and the Chinese delegation?'

Jackal was staring at Rahul like he'd never seen him before. This cut-throat business mogul role was brand new and suited him. He quickly looked through the documents, realizing Rahul was right and that he, Jackal as the patent owner would be getting a comfortable royalty for life. The offer made to the Chinese was also better than industry standard, by a little margin, but nevertheless, lower than what they had quoted. Keeping in mind the reasons Rahul had just spoken of, he looked over at the Chinese MD and spoke to him in Chinese, telling him in no uncertain terms, that this was probably the best they could hope for and that he knew Rahul Bhatia by reputation, they wouldn't be getting a better offer than this.

During this time, Rajesh spoke quietly to Rahul, 'I don't know whether they will go for it. We've very steeply under quoted what the Chinese were looking for. Although, they did not know about the patents. When did that happen?'

'It'll happen. Don't worry. And, I asked our team to look over the application of the tech and if there was a way to patent it, yesterday when I was going through the files. It was open, so they applied for it, with my consent. Hope that was okay? I told them you would be okay with it.'

After a further five minutes of to and fro between Jackal and the Chinese, with the Indian delegation patiently waiting, the Chinese MD stood up to shake hands with Rahul and confirm in broken English that it would be his pleasure to accept the terms offered by them.

His father clapped him on the back as he sat back down and grinned. He then pointed at Jackal and said quietly, 'Papa, meet Jackal.' His father's eyes widened with sudden recall of the name, as he and the foreign delegates were then swooped down upon by the M&A team to get all the documents signed and sealed.

The Circle Bar
Crowne Plaza, Johannesburg

The famous haunt of the rich and elite was filling up with what looked like the who's who of Johannesburg, though it was still early. The ambient lighting and the wood panel bar offered a mix of club and chill vibes. It would turn into a full-fledged dance club in a few hours' time.

Jackal and Rahul found space in the VIP section of the bar and were being waited upon, instead of the norm of self service. *Money, makes all things possible, thought Jackal.*

He was looking at Rahul trying to figure out what the difference was. He hadn't changed much with regards his looks, maybe become more handsome, but there was an ease to him, and he was curious. He mentioned this thoughts to Rahul inquiringly.

Rahul laughed, 'Just sorted out my life a bit.'

They spent the next few hours catching up on each other's life's experiences. Jackal told him about leaving college to move to the US for his research work, and apologized for disappearing on them. He said, as of date he had 207 patents to his name and that the Chinese had come looking for him a couple of years ago. He had his fingers in pies across the world, in some of the biggest and some of the niche industries and business of the world. Rahul thumped him on the back with pride and told him so verbally too, that he was glad, for America and China apparently gave him more opportunities than India ever could have done. He then proceeded to inform Jackal about Rehan and Ritesh. Jackal said he knew about Ritesh as he had a google alert set on all three of them, to stay updated with their news. He felt terrible about missing Ritesh's funeral and the last few years since they graduated from college. Rahul patted Jackal's shoulder as he dealt with Ritesh's death afresh. Rahul who had done his share of weeping was now in a position to accept Ritesh's loss and carry his light within his heart. He reminded Jackal of Ritesh's vision in life and hugged him. Jackal calmed down a little and raised his glass to toast Ritesh's life.

After a lengthy silence, he turned to Rahul and said, 'I have something to tell you.'

CHAPTER 17

―⚍―

Bhiwadi, Rajasthan

Rehan had brought Swapnil to one of his favourite parks in Bhiwadi. Nestled in a relatively sleepy part of what was now a full-fledged industrial town, this oasis of greenery was where Rehan's father used to bring him as a child. There was a large, sturdy banyan tree which served as Rehan's playground, ever since he could remember. His father taught him how to climb a tree, just like he was now teaching Swapnil.

He remembered the days gone by when his dad used to climb up to the highest sturdiest branch he could find, and then call Rehan up. He used to stand, on the thick inner branches with his arms around his father, looking out at the yet barren city.

His dad used to talk about the future here as they saw Bhiwadi transform from patchy green and somewhat dusty landscapes into concrete dwellings. The town smoked its way into the glory and prosperity—new industries, new jobs, prosperity and growing real estate were the proof.

His vision focused nearer now, as he looked at little Swapnil running amok in the garden, pretending to be an airplane, while holding the model airplane he had picked up at the station on his way back from Delhi last week. Hearing

Swapnil's laughter was a soothing balm to his antsy soul. His thoughts drifting again... *What is the purpose of the life we are born into? Do we decide it? Or, is it predestined? Are we mere pawns in the hands of destiny? Can we design our own destiny? Why do we make the choices we make? Is there free will?*

Abba, you wanted me to stay back here and contribute to the growth of my home town. I did that, I contributed. But now, I feel so empty within. Your death shook me and Ritesh's death has broken me. He was a man who lived and died by what he believed in. Am I doing what I believe to be is true? I feel so incomplete.'

He closed his eyes.

Why are people weak? What holds us back from having a solid backbone and dealing with our adversities head on? Why are the repercussions of each action based on those around us? Why are we not just limited to ourselves? And inversely, if we are to live for others...then why is it one way at times? How does one's soul feed itself when all you're doing is feeding someone else's?

Why does Swapnil have to live with his parents' decision to discard him? Why is he now living with my decision? Who's writing his destiny? Am I? Is he?

Rehan's questions faded into the soft rays of the setting sun when he opened his doe brown eyes.

Saint Pal Orphanage, Bhiwadi

Rehan had brought Swapnil back to the orphanage for one of his weekly weekend duties—storytime. As big a fan he was of comic books and animated characters, he felt that all kids, especially these kids should have a chance at feeling the thrill of a life so far imagined—a preview into new worlds, culture, people and stories.

He was surrounded by a group of children, listening to him voice the end of another story where the bad guy is defeated by the good and righteous superhero—today's was Spiderman. Some days it was a reading of international classics by *Marvel* or *DC*, and some days it was *Amar Chitra Katha*; a steady mix of two very different worlds; one foreign and one their own.

The boys and girls were sitting in assorted poses; some lying down on the ground, some with their feet against the wall, some just sitting with their legs crossed beneath them as they stared at their Rehan bhaiya. As he finished the night's story, a group of them started acting like the supervillains and superheroes they had heard of. Rehan was looking around at them, revelling in their infectious grins when he noticed the headlights of a car approaching the orphanage.

All the kids stopped playing to stare at the newcomers. With the headlights at full beam, all the kids and Rehan could see were two silhouettes, kicking up the dust as they walked towards them through the open gates.

Rehan recognized Rahul immediately. He could distinguish his best friend's walk anywhere in the world. He stood up unhurriedly and walked down the three steps to the ground. Rahul bounded up in his casuals, his norm when not working, his trademark black denims and a shirt and hugged Rehan. Rehan, pleasantly surprised, asked him if he got his plane ticket mixed up.

'*Jaana tha Boston, pahunch gaye Bhiwadi*, eh brother? What's up? All good?'

Rahul laughed out loud, 'Better than good bro! Better than awesome. Look who I've got for you.'

Rehan peered past Rahul and his eyes widened. Wearing what could only be described as a smoky velvet tuxedo with expensive shoes and carrying a leather man-purse, walking with a majestic strut, was Jai Kishan Amre, a stark contrast to where he was standing. This was opulent to the point of overdone. Rehan laughed out loud. He went forward and hugged Jackal.

'Dr Jackal! Woah man! How did you find him?' Rehan asked Rahul, while thumping Jackal's back.

'Where the hell have you been man? You disappeared without a trace. Damn! It's so good to see you buddy...,' he directed towards Jackal as Rahul shrugged.

'That's a long story, Rehan...,' Jackal was interrupted by the gang of children who ran up to hug both the newcomers.

'You look like a hero! You look like a villain. Are you? Are you superheroes? Do...,' Rehan quickly shuffled the kids firing the questions back inside, promising them that the two bhaiyas will be back soon, but now was bedtime. He handed over the charge back to Sitaram chacha and bid him adieu.

Rehan's Home, Later That Evening

'Where did you go Jackal? We didn't even get a chance to wish you goodbye and good luck, not that you needed it, yeah? You look like you're doing well,' Rehan said a while later. He had introduced Jackal to his ammi and was now waiting to hear what had been happening over the past half decade since college.

Ammi placed the tray bearing tea and snacks on the table in front of them. Rahul said, 'Aree, ammi, we'll manage. *Aap aao*. Sit down here.' He pointed to the charpai in the courtyard where they were all sitting and as she did, he promptly lay his head down on her lap.

Jackal looked at the loving caresses Rahul was receiving from Rehan's ammi. He looked at them enviously for a second before picking up a cup of chai for himself and answering Rehan, 'Yaar, you know, I'm really bad at goodbyes. And I loved you three. I couldn't deal with it. The company that had hired me for my research sent me to America the very next day, so I had to go home and pack. Things were also not good with family at that time, so when I got the opportunity to run away, I did.'

'We get it...,' Rahul spoke up. 'Family situations make you do things that you may or may not have done generally.'

Rehan nodded, 'but it would have been good to see you once before you'd left...'

Looking solemnly at Rehan and Rahul, Jackal replied, 'If I get to do it over, I still would have left you know.'

Rahul and Rehan both looked at Jackal, surprised, and then exchanged a glance that had them bursting out laughing.

'You're such a brilliantly eccentric dude!' Rehan exclaimed.

'Wait for it bro...you don't know half of how brilliant he is,' Rahul exclaimed.

They had just finished with dinner and were clearing the plates when Rehan said with a staggered surprise, 'What you guys are talking is huge.'

'Yes it is,' nodded Jackal.

'And so is every revolution. It starts with a strong resolution in here and a hell lot of GMD,' Rahul's eyes twinkled as he pointed at his heart.

'Are you in?' Jackal looked inquiringly at Rehan.

Rehan looked up at the night sky, recalling his thoughts from earlier that day. It seemed like days ago when he sat at the park with Swapnil thinking of the future and what it held for them, the destiny they lived by; and here, in just a span of a few hours, he was being given a chance to inscribe his own path.

Rehana looked at her son. She knew the angst and guilt that had troubled Rehan for the past few years and more so after Ritesh's death. The path set by his abbu versus the light his heart was showing had halted his steps in life. She knew now it was time. She put her hand on his shoulders and urged him along.

'It's time for you to complete your dream, jaana, your abba wanted you to work for and work with your people. Help them change their lives with your talent. By doing this you will be able to fulfil your mission in a bigger and better way, set your own path jaana. Your abba will always be proud of you.'

Rehan felt like this was what he was waiting for. He was doing his bit in social work while working in his home town. But with something like this he felt complete. He would be able to live up to his father's dream in a perfect way. He stood up suddenly, radiating energy and a new zeal for life. He turned towards his friends and pulled them up too. He placed his palm facing up between the three of them; Rahul and Jackal too put their hands in Rehan's and hi-fived each other.

'Right, that's that then,' said Jackal, 'There's just one more thing. We need to head to Delhi, where you will meet our last but not the least, fourth member of the core team.'

'What?' Rahul questioned. 'We have one more member?'

'Yep.'

'Why?'

'For a few reasons—one, we're three dudes with a crazy idea, we need to have a balance, someone to keep us grounded, two; we need someone with an aesthetic sense to match our engineering degrees, three; for what we've planned, we'll need the feminine energy and edge.'

'Who is it?'

'You'll see.'

Gurgaon-Faridabad Road

The Mercedes SUV was speeding down the eight lane highway. The route, so familiar yet was so different for the four occupants of the car. All four, were lost in their thoughts as the car sped down the gravel road towards Manav Sanrachna University. Jackal, who had called shot-gun was looking out of his window, his excitement building with every passing milestone. Behind him, Rehan too, was gazing out at the landscape, thinking about their destination, and how every time they rode to college, he was on Ritesh's bike, his co passenger.

Rahul was looking at the road, his eyes hidden behind his trademark aviators, hands on the steering, charting the course to their college. Not for a lack of trying did his eyes keep wandering to the passenger behind him; wearing a modest kurti over jeans. His mind took him back to a couple of evenings ago, when Jackal invited the fourth member of their quad to his house. Jor Bagh would serve as HQ for a while till they sourced out a new place for their work.

'Jackal, who is this fourth member? What's with the mystery?' Rehan had asked again as they unloaded their bags from Rahul's car.

'It's a mystery only for a short while longer, dudes. I've called our fourth member over today evening. I hope you don't mind, Rahul,' Jackal said.

While he had nonchalantly shaken his head, he had been curious.

A few hours later, Rahul's and Rehan's curiosity was assuaged, their jaws dropping open in surprise when they saw who it was that Jackal had invited to Rahul's house.

Neha Khare had walked in, escorted by an enthusiastic Jackal who had gone out to receive her at the gate. Her persona and style had changed, grown, as she had; no more just a girl, but a woman. Her clothing style too displayed her confident, strong aura. She had adorned stylish pants and a straight cut kurta over it with a beaded neckpiece. Her hair was still long, and swept to one side. She looked at Rahul, as though she had walked out of a fashion spread, straight into his living room; more beautiful than he remembered in his memories. That glimpse during Ritesh's funeral, in the rain, didn't do her any justice. She was more breathtaking now than she was even in college.

Rehan had gotten up and walked halfway across the room to hug and welcome her, making his surprise and delight very evident. *Lucky bastard.*

Rahul had stood up after what seemed like an eternity and stammered out a welcome, swallowing that big lump in his throat, as the three stared at him. *Why was the universe bringing Neha back into his life now? What was the meaning of this? What was the point?*

Over the next 90 minutes, Jackal had informed them of how he had kept in touch with Neha over the years. This had brought about many teasing remarks from Rehan about how Jackal chose to stay connected to Neha versus them, his best friends for four years. Jackal had blushed red, hurriedly changing the topic.

'To be fair, we only connected a few years ago. I had read an article about biochemical research that I remembered Jackal used to be into, so I sent an email to him with a link. I didn't know that his old email id would still work or even that he would recall who I was. But as it turned out, that research was being headed by him, and he did remember me...' she had broken off, her eyes on Rahul.

Rahul remained silent for most of the evening, speaking only when prompted to; except for one instance. Jackal told them about the current stage they were at and if they were to begin, how and when it would be plausible. The team got together and mapped out a rough timeline about how things should proceed. Rehan was again on leave; he had to give his notice to the office and was wondering how to go about it. He couldn't afford to leave his job, nor could he afford to offer one month's notice. Jackal had assured them that he had no other full-time assignments and was free to take on whatever his heart desired. Rahul too had clarified where he stood, work wise.

Jackal had gone for a loo break when Rahul spoke up and addressed Neha, for the first time. 'Why do you want to be a part of this?' his tone half annoyed, half curious.

Neha and Rehan both had looked up with surprise. Rehan had started shaking his head then, and Neha... Neha had just looked at him with this calm smile on her face, 'I have many reasons Rahul, but I'll tell you the ones that'll make sense to you right now. One, I have been involved with the ideation of this project since over a year ago when Jackal first proposed it to me. I had shown my inclination towards it and my interest. Two, if we go about doing it the way we've projected you will need my expertise. If you remember I have a background in Electronics Engineering but beyond that I went and further got a degree in interiors and urban planning which gives me the exact requisites for this job. Three, I knew and respected Ritesh as much as the next person, and this dream that we're all dreaming in his honour, is something I wouldn't give up for anything in the world. Four, if you really must know, I care and want to do something for this country. I really do, and that's why when I got this opportunity, I held on to it with both hands. There are a couple of more reasons Rahul...but the time is not right for me to disclose them now.'

Rahul looking down at his shoes had murmured thanks, while Rehan had been looking at Neha in awe, telling her how brilliant it is that she's part of the core team. And Jackal had come back and diffused the situation with talk of food and drinks.

Back in the car, Rahul was looking at Neha through the rear-view mirror. She was glancing out at the scenery, seemingly lost in her thoughts.

He realized that he would have to talk to Neha one on one to avoid this uneasiness between them, but when that would happen was something he had to figure out. *I don't even know where to start.*

'We're here,' Jackal pointed out as the gates of MSU became visible in the afternoon haze.

'It feels so odd, walking in here without Ritesh,' Rahul said softly.

'But can't you feel him around you?' Rehan asked gently, 'His energy binds us together. It was a good idea Jackal, to start here.'

Neha glanced at Rahul as they walked in through the hallowed gates of their alma mater.

This is where we started...

Feeling Neha's gaze on himself, Rahul steeled himself to look at her as they walked past the central park.

This is also where we ended...

'Come, we need to go to the lab. I'd already spoken to the lab assistant.'

'Apart from the nostalgia obviously, Jackal, why did we need to come to college for the lab?' inquired Rahul.

'Ah! My dear friend, I thought you might have known already. Look, what we're discussing here is a crazy but as yet, not a patented idea. If I were to show you what I'm planning in any commercial lab, there are chances of it being heard, recorded or even copied. Our college lab on the other hand, is going to be empty today evening and we will have complete privacy.'

They had reached the lab and Jackal was being called by the old lab attendant. Even after so many years, he recognized Jackal's distinctive features instantly. He had been his favourite student, often coming to tinkle around in the lab after hours, doing his own thing. He spent a lot of evenings having chai with this curious young kid.

'Dada can we use this lab for a few hours?' Jackal asked softly.

'It was always yours beta.'

Four Hours Later

'Jackal, what you are showing us is revolutionary. It will change the existing landscape forever,' Rehan said excitedly as they walked out of the lab.

'You are a genius. If we can pull this off, it'll be...' Rahul hugged Jackal.

'Brilliant,' Neha completed.

On stepping out of the lab they saw the twinkling lights of the canteen in the distance calling out to them like when they were students here. All four of them were transported back to the days when a random discussion would turn into an impromptu lecture or debate session. Ritesh, though never inclined towards politics was always brought to the fore. He was the unofficial valedictorian of their batch. Seniors and juniors alike used to look up to him voicing his opinions on the latest in the political, cultural and life's happenstance. He used to be a great orator, great thinker, and yet, great listener too. He used to instigate debates that made people think, really use their senses to come up with logical and emotional ideas, and not just pass life by.

The core team walked into the canteen, nothing much had changed in the last so many years; apart from the addition of more buildings that held more modernized cafeterias. To this quad though, this original canteen had all the flavours,

The Amigos

all the memories. They walked past the round tables to their reserved table.

'I have one more thing for you guys…' Jackal looked at the three people accompanying him. 'Especially since we're here, I thought it might be fitting to…' his voice faded off as he rummaged in his man-purse for something.

Rahul, Rehan and Neha looked at each other with confusion writ on their faces.

'What…' started Rahul.

'You guys remember I used to cart around a recorder in our last year? Well, I…I can't explain. Just listen. You'll understand.'

He placed a small Apple dock on the table in front of them, and tapped his iPhone.

It's like they were back in 2006 and Ritesh's voice filled the canteen.

Gee Mein Dee, GMD, guys. Do you have it in you?

You will wonder what is GMD. Some will laugh because you think you know what gaali I'm referring to. It's not that. Let me tell you, the definition of GMD is unique for every individual. It is not what you think the letters abbreviate to.

We all dream right? We all desire that one thing we want to make true. Everyone here is nurturing a dream deep inside their hearts…but let me ask you, how many of you actually go ahead and do it? How many of us have the courage to follow our heart? How many of us have the GMD to stand up and prove our convictions? Your dream can be anything, A housewife can dream of being a dancer, a corporate honcho can dream of being a singer, a young student can dream of being an owner of a restaurant or being an owner of an IT enterprise. Maybe you engineering guys don't want to be in engineering, but out dancing, or creating art or cooking in the best restaurant in France, or joining the army or even standing up to what is right. Hell, maybe for you, following what your family wants you to do is what requires GMD, maybe they're the ones that are rebels, making you question your life. Each to his own. Each person will define GMD in their own context.

Since we're talking about this, these dreams can be about your interpersonal relationships, it can be about your career choices, it can be standing up for the country, it can be your whole being—the way you are.

Your brain may not lead you on the path towards your dreams. Most dreams die because your brain listens to convention and tried and tested methods, it find the easy way out, following in the footsteps of those that have done it earlier. What about following your heart?

Keep your hand on your heart and answer me. Do we all follow our hearts?

Do we?

I can't hear any answers... You know why? Because, you've never thought about it as your choice. It's everyone's choice, except yours. Right? Some brave souls here would say, yes they follow their dreams, and I salute them. Thank God for people like you. I hope you're being honest with yourself and not just placating yourself, ki haan, bhai, I do what I want. No, it's so much more than what you want in the moment. It's what you desire, from the deepest part of you, when your heart, soul, and brain combine and aim towards that one thing or two, or few.

It is so easy, to let someone else decide. To let someone else make decisions for you and tell you what is right and wrong, what you should do and not do, what or who you should follow or not follow, how you should live or not live, how you should talk or not talk. It's simple because, of so many reasons:

One, you don't need to think. Two, if something goes wrong, you can turn around and blame the person who told you to do things a certain way. No responsibility like that. Yeah? Three, it's how the world has been functioning. Our generation, the guys before us, and the generation before them, and so on. Dastoor hai, duniya ka. What a joke! The fourth reason is that it's safe. SAFE! Safe to follow. An option where you don't need a soul. You don't need life within. A 'lifeless' person will tread the path that is already explored by others but a person who is full of life will have the GMD to follow the path where his or her heart takes them.

To follow your heart, you have to have rebellious streak. But society hates rebellion. At the very core of its foundation, society is formed to kill rebels and stop them from taking root. Because society is about order, and order would come when you control people, when you put people in slots. She is like this, she can only be this. He is like that he can only be like that. Your family is this, you can only do this.

But rebels cannot be slotted. They create their own way and follow it with passion. Rebels are those that dream. And not just dream, but make it a reality.

You know what dreams are like today? What required GMD? Dum is when you say NO to a corrupt official asking for bribe. Dum is when you take picture of your stalker and post it in a social website. Dum is when you tell a person to stop throwing litter on the road or at a railway station. Dum is also when you provide a helping hand to a blind man crossing the road. Dum is when you save a girl from eve teasing, hell, GMD in today's world is also keeping your own hands off a girl, no matter what state she is in. Basic humanity, the core of humanity, is what GMD is all about now.

GMD hona matlab jeena. More than just existing. It's living. Living each moment to the absolute fullest. Do you have a dream for yourself? I ask you again? Do you have a dream?

If you don't have a dream for yourself, do you have one for someone else? Is there any way you can make someone else's life better? If being selfless towards a cause, or towards someone else, means GMD hona, then yes, you have it.

Step away from the mundane. Choose to live. Choose your love. Choose your desires. Choose passion. And turn it into your life.

GMD is that belief to follow your heart. It is that courage to stand up and say 'NO, I will not do what I don't believe in. I will follow my heart.' And your heart will never lead you on the wrong path. It takes GMD to stand up to your loved ones and your well-wishers and your seniors and tell them that you want to do what your heart desires, instead of the normal, boring, steady choices they offer. So tomorrow, when you decide for yourself, what you want to do in life, how you want your universe to be, how you want people to remember you... Yaar, gunday mat banjana. Hahaha.

But on a serious note, you have to decide, whether you have GMD or not.

And if you ask me, I'll tell you, each one of you has GMD. All you have to do is look deep within yourself and accept it. When does your heart know that what it's doing is right? When the brain and soul follow and support.

Find it guys. Find the GMD within you...'

Ritesh had ended his talk to loud cheers and applause and whistles as he jumped down from the table he was standing on and sank into his chair next to Rahul and Rehan.

—⁂—

Today, sitting at the same table, Rehan, Rahul, Jackal and Neha, all felt like they were being enveloped in a warm embrace by Ritesh. His words adding fuel to the kindling they were starting, in his name.

They felt Ritesh's words reverberating in their blood, the fire shown in their eyes...this GMD was going to revolutionize their lives, and those who they touched.

CHAPTER 18

Six Months Later

*Shop Floor, Bhatia Steel Factory Annex,
Industrial Area, Delhi*

Rehan was overseeing phase three of the process. Every step of the design had to be followed very carefully. The spark of creation emanating when one hot metal collided with another component, every such union brought a satisfactory smile to his face.

An engineer's craft is best exhibited on the proximity of the final product with the original design.

The blueprint of the design was created by both Neha and Jackal. The conversions from design ideas to 3D renderings and shop floor management was being taken care of by him, since he had hands on experience for five years doing exactly this for Mahadev Industries. It had taken them six months to get the existing machines modified and new ones designed to the exact specifications that they required. Today, the first prototype would be created.

They had spent endless hours over the past six months finalizing every line of design, every angle and curvature. There were debates, there were disagreements but it was finally concluded with something which was ingenious and would be looked upon as a milestone in the history and future of creative inventions.

Rahul came up behind Rehan and clapped him on the back. 'How's it going buddy? On track so far?'

Rehan took off his safety glasses and nodded as he walked back into the cabin overlooking the machine room.

'What's up with you? Done with your meetings?' Rehan countered as they climbed up the wrought iron staircase to the air conditioned room behind the glass enclosure.

'Yeah man, satisfactory meeting. Land acquisition is not the easiest thing to do in our country. You have to take permissions from gram panchayats, you have government agencies loaded with bureaucratic policies. It's not exactly a cakewalk. Shitty work.'

'What was the final outcome? Are we on track with our deadlines?'

'Well, sort of. So far. This was the prelim meeting with a few panchayat members and the third consecutive meeting with the rest of them. Bhoj is turning out to be very helpful...'

'Pankaj Bhoj?' interrupted Rehan. 'How is he helping?'

'You know he is a MLA now, and his family goes a long way back into politics. One of his uncles turned out to be a member of the panchayat. So not only is he helping us out there, but he's using his position to get the red tape and paperwork moved on time, otherwise we'd be waiting for months before some sarkari babu even looks at our petitions. No bribes, just efficient working. Very surprising, coming from Bhoj actually. Haha.' Rahul laughed.

Rehan looked impressed.

'Jackal and I went with Bhoj and explained to them today, again, what we're planning and what it could potentially mean. By the end of it they were amazed, but I'm sure were wondering whether we would be able to pull it off.'

'Hi boys,' Neha called out as she walked into the room. 'Jackal's just given me an update on the meeting. Congratulations. He also mentioned you have food! I'm starving!' She pointed first at Rahul and then herself, and sat down on the only end of the table that didn't have papers and folders strewn all over.

'Seriously Rehan, you need an assistant to manage all this for you.' she said, helping herself to the food box that Rahul had placed on the table earlier. His lunch, along with that for the team was delivered from home every day. Since Rehan has essentially moved into his house and Jackal had rented out a flat he barely went to, spending most of his waking hours in the makeshift lab created for him in the empty room, it fell upon Rahul to provide food for them. Neha too had given up her other freelance contracting jobs and was focusing on this one, full time.

Rehan, busy with a few last minute checks on inventory for the prototype was busy at his computer and the phone, confirming with technicians downstairs about availability, missed the awkward glances between Neha and Rahul. She had positioned herself directly in front of Rahul, sitting a couple of feet away. As was the norm over the past six months, when they were not discussing business, the silence between them became fraught with awkwardness, which led to...

Rahul got up and hurriedly walked out, muttering, 'enjoy your lunch' under his breath.

Rehan looked up after a minute and saw Neha looking forlorn, 'Where's Rahul?' he asked.

Neha shrugged, looking down at her phone.

Rehan understood what must have happened. *As usual. Idiots both of them.*

'Neha, can I talk to you about something personal? If you don't mind?'

She looked up at him and shrugged again.

'One of the reasons you came back was because of him right? You wanted to give this another shot? Or are you just waiting for an apology?' he asked softly.

Neha looked at Rehan for a second before replying with a sad smile, 'You are way too clever for your own good Mr Khan...I...it's not an apology I want anymore... Not in the way you, or anyone else might think.'

Rehan sat down behind the desk as Neha got up and started pacing. He looked at her over his steepled fingers, 'Explain,' he said.

'You're close to Rahul. You must know what happened, right?'

'I want to hear from you Neha. Yeah, I won't deny having an idea, but I'd like to know from your point of view.'

Neha looked straight at Rehan. She could feel he genuinely cared, his honesty and sincerity showed in his face; and so she took a deep breath and recalled some of her best and worst days.

'Look, Rehan, you know how it was like between Rahul and me. We were both so temperamental and full of attitude, and even though we had a rocky start with his stupid tricks trying to impress me with his running skills, I genuinely fell for him during that time when you guys fought with Pankaj. That's when I had realized that there is more to Rahul than just a pretty face and an attitude; I got to know he had a heart too, and that he cared deeply about issues and situations. In your last year, and my first, he and I became close. Mind you, he had not asked me to be his girlfriend or anything, nothing official, but we were together.'

'You remember, I'd come to your farewell party? I wanted to be part of his special day; the last proper occasion we would have, since you guys were leaving college post that. That night...that night I did not expect or anticipate what Rahul would do. I wasn't then and still am not the kind of girl who will make out with anyone or anytime or...Rahul, he crossed his limits that night. Forcing himself onto me when I wasn't ready for it; that wasn't what I was looking for.' She continued, 'I couldn't then give him what he wanted. You guys were barely going to be there for another month. Rahul was talking of moving outside Delhi, wherever he would get a job. He didn't even try applying to places in Delhi NCR. How were we supposed to be in a relationship or something if he was leaving?' She looked at Rehan listening to her narration with complete intensity.

'That night, after... he told me he loved me, and that he was showing me love when he did that. One, physicality is not the only way to show someone you love them, forcing it is definitely not how you do it. Two, telling someone you love them is very easy, it's what comes next that is the difficult part. It's one thing to tell someone you love, it's completely different to conform by that love. He didn't get it. He would have disappeared from my life. He was in any case leaving college, and I was only starting it. I couldn't have left it for four years, and he never wanted to come back. Where would that have left us? Or our relationship?' She paused for second and said. 'Later that night, Rahul became this mad person. Do you remember how he beat up Nitin? He was behaving like a mad guy. Between all of that, he kept pushing me here and there. I couldn't deal with it. I didn't know what to think. I was shocked. Ritesh...Ritesh had taken care of all of that after you took Rahul back to the hostel. He apologized to everyone. He ensured that Nitin was okay. He came with us to the infirmary; he made sure Nitin was fine, before finding someone to send me home. But mostly everyone was drunk by then and he thought it might not be good to send me back to Delhi in the middle of the night, so he asked Shruti from your batch to take me to her hostel room and make sure I was okay. He walked me back to the hostel, apologized for Rahul's behaviour, and explained everything. But, I couldn't understand anything then. It took me a lot of years to get over how Rahul behaved that night. I thought he was the guy he was with you and Ritesh, but as it turned out, he acted like the jerk I had tried avoiding in the beginning. I was so confused about him, that night. Which was the real Rahul?'

'I did expect Rahul to get in touch at least once, the next day or the next week, or even after his exams, to explain, or apologize or even just say goodbye, but instead, he just disappeared. And so, I came to realize that maybe what happened had to happen. That's how our destiny played with us...I'm sure he too has his version of how he saw things that night, I'll give him the benefit of doubt, but I can't assume. Today, he doesn't even look me in the eye; now is that because he hates me for not doing what he was forcing me to or because he's apologetic? I don't know, and never will I guess, so it leaves us at an impasse.'

After a short pause, she continued, 'I always respected Ritesh and when I heard about his death, I came to pay my respects at his funeral. I...I had thought you guys might be there but didn't know what I would do if I met Rahul, or how it would happen. In any case, it was inevitable I guess, because Jackal, who had been in touch with me all these years, sent me a message that he met Rahul in Johannesburg and that he was going to involve you guys in the idea. And so here we are...' She finished, looking straight at Rehan's big brown empathetic eyes. Rehan looked at Neha kindly, feeling like a protective brother.

'Thank you for telling me your story... Can I ask you one more question?'

Neha laughed lightly and nodded, 'Go on.'

'Do you still like him?'

She smiled at Rehan, 'Time will tell...'

CHAPTER 19

2016
GMD Enterprises Pvt Ltd

Rajesh Bhatia walked along a long gallery leading to the plush reception area of the private offices of the Board of Directors of GMD Enterprises and the ensuite common conference room. The gallery was lined with larger than life blow ups of black and white photos, showcasing and detailing a journey captured over the past five years.

Anyone that entered the office, had to walk through this gallery; the artery that led off to various different departmental offices via hidden passages. The interiors and the building itself were an architectural marvel, but even so, it was the photographs that made people stop.

One of the very first photographs was that of a group of people—three boys and a girl, standing on the roof of a SUV, overlooking a barren spot of land, captioned '75 Acres of Revolution'.

The next canvas captioned 'The Groundbreaking' was a collage of pictures—one captured the slight dust storm created by the line of trucks driving into the area, one picture was a row of JCB Earthmovers with their buckets raised as though in a salute. Another picture caught the smiles of a group of villagers as they watched the machines moving through their lands.

As he moved down the corridor, his eyes glanced at the canvases showing the group of four laying down the foundation stones surrounded by applauding villagers. The next one was the inverse, where a few women from the village and their children laid the foundation stones and were applauded by the co-founders of this enterprise.

By the time he reached the end of the gallery, he like every guest, had the sense of living through the journey—of the first factory, the second unit, the first installation, the first success, the rise and empowerment that it offered, the changes in the landscape of an old barren land in the middle of nowhere. Right at the end though, there was a candid picture of a group of five college kids, four boys and a girl, dressed casually and laughing at something, in the midst of a group hi five. This backlit picture was titled 'GMD—Do you have it in you?' and scribbled below that were five names—Jackal, Rehan, Ritesh, Rahul and Neha.

Even though he had been here many times in the past five years, these pictures still touched him and added a sense of wonder and pride. He had all but adopted the four youngsters, and felt proud in being their mentor from time to time.

Today was a special day. It was barely half past seven in the morning, but he knew that the team would be in office. From day one, Rahul, Rehan, Jai Kishan and Neha had to be forced to leave the office or the plant from time to time, but they were back as soon as they could manage. He had had a bittersweet moment where Rahul had to resign from the day to day workings of Bhatia Steel, but extremely proud of his son's dedication and work ethic. His son had the same zeal and conviction to succeed in him that he himself had and his father had. He was glad to see his son accepting his name and his blood and pouring himself into something he diligently believed in.

But I digress, he thought as he crossed the carpeted and beautifully designed reception area to get to his son's office. He knew they wouldn't have seen it yet. His excitement knew no bounds.

'What's up Dad?' Rahul asked, surprised to see his father walk in this early. The team was huddled around a blueprint for a new set up on the outskirts of Punjab. They had a meeting with the Punjab State Government in a couple of weeks for which they needed to prepare.

'Good morning, Rajesh uncle,' a chorus went around the conference room table.

'You look way too excited for this time of day uncle, What's up?' Neha prompted.

'Beta, here you go,' Rajesh tossed one newspaper and one magazine on to the table.

Jackal and Rehan hurried to the other side. Rahul casually picked up the magazine in front of him.

'The *Indian Express* and *TIME* magazine, both have given you extensive coverage regarding your enterprise and nominations. Your interview is a full-page article and photos splashed all over them, and they're brilliant!' Rajesh exclaimed.

'Wow dad!' Rahul let out a low whistle, 'Didn't expect it to be this amazing.'

'Wohoo!' Jackal and Rehan couldn't stop pumping the air while attempting to read the coverage in *The Indian Express*.

'Holy crap!' Neha said as she read over Rahul's shoulder and saw photographs of all four of them and that of the plant.

'It has been a long time coming, kids.'

'I mean...we've had articles out before, smaller ones that give us a mention, but damn! *TIME*!! Did we give them an interview too?' Rahul asked.

Rehan shook his head, 'Nope, Amber? The PR intern, this summer, she arranged for some press releases to be sent out. She mentioned she was contacting magazines and setting up interviews, but I don't recall which ones. Maybe it was *TIME*. Wow. We might need to hire her permanently.'

'Oh, wait, I have an email from her that I glanced at...Let me...' Neha quickly pulled out her phone and scrolled down to the email. 'Yep, I marked it as important, but didn't go into the details. She was to meet me today to discuss it. They've asked for an interview. They want to do a cover story on us. Holy shit.'

She looked up and saw the four men staring at her. She mirrored their expressions of disbelief, 'Wow.'

'Things are really happening, aren't they?' Rahul asked all of them.

Jackal replied, 'Guys hold on,' he took his tab out, found the article online and put it up on the projector.

THE INDIAN EXPRESS

An Electrifying New Idea

A New-Age Patent for Creating Energy

Alwar Goswami, Harchandpur, Rajasthan
New Delhi, April 19 2016, 2.02 a.m.

'They say it takes one to bring about change in the world, and here are four of us, working as one, to do exactly that,' Jai Kishan Amre, one of the four Directors at GMD Enterprises, responsible for Innovation, R&D and Technicals, starts off the introductions as we drive towards the 75-acre plant.

The newly reconstructed National Highway 24 B is lined with utility poles after utility poles. On questioning if this leads to and from their plant, they candidly nod. (Picture Inset)

This is a profile as an introduction to this year's nominee for 'The Express India Inc Awards'.

GMD Enterprises started operations five years ago, and is a new entrant in the energy and power field, going up against established giants. They deal with the production and distribution of solar energy. While the idea of solar energy being tapped and converted to electricity is not a new one by any means, it is the patented technology at GMD Enterprises that makes it truly novel.

'It's ingenuity lies in the design of the solar panel and the materials used in the production of solar cells. We have taken the ordinary to exceptional at half the cost.' Rahul Bhatia, Director, GMD Enterprises, appraising the role of Government & Private Liaoning.

Mr Amre explains the science behind their technology, 'About 60 per cent of the light that hits the Earth's surface is visible light. The rest lies in the infrared spectrum, think night vision goggles, the ones they show in Hollywood action movies. The other part of this sunlight consists of the ultraviolet spectrum, think sunburn, like, when we go to the beach and expose our skin to the sun. During my college days, when I first started researching the biology of the sun's energy, it often led to me explore desolated areas and study the numerous patterns and amounts of light getting absorbed by different particles and species of flora at different places. During my masters program at the University of Texas, I went ahead and carried out an experimental research resulting in the development of a prototype of a new carbon-based solar panel. Our traditional silicon-based solar photovoltaic cells can only convert visible light into energy, thus leaving huge amounts of potential energy untapped. The solar panel we have created can harness the light in the infrared range also. These new carbon cells are transparent, meaning they could be transposed on top of existing silicon-based cells to gather both infrared and visible sunlight and harness the complete energy being emitted by the sun.'

While Mr Amre created the first of these cells, converting them into a village full of solar panels fell upon the very capable shoulders of Mr Rehan Khan, Director, Supply Chain & Production. 'The cells are made of carbon nanotubes which are highly absorbent while needing very little material, which makes it highly cost effective. In simple terms, our carbon based solar cells tap and hence generate more energy, almost close to 40 per cent more than any other conventional solar set up, making our plant one of the most productive and profitable plants in the country.'

'What makes our enterprise truly special is that these solar panels have been integrated into the rooftops of all the houses of the village Harchandpur near Bhiwadi. Hence the entire village has become a solar plant for us. We have named them "Building-Integrated Photovoltaic Cell". They are installed not only on the rooftops of the houses but even the window panels are also made of these solar panels and collaborate in generating the electricity. These integrated photovoltaics cut out many installation costs as they don't require racking, which means the labourers don't need necessarily need to be trained in solar installations.'

Mr Bhatia adds, 'It is because of this that we are able to tap and hence generate more energy and effectively sell it back to Government, who uses this renewable energy in nearby areas which previously had severe electricity shortage. Over the past year, the surrounding villages and towns use electricity produced at our plant. The electricity bill of the entire region has become more cost effective by upto 75 per cent.'

'Setting up this plant in a relatively undeveloped area and converting an entire village into a self-sufficient solar plant was not the only distinctive thought that we started this project with. Over 90 per cent of active workers in our SPV (solar plant village) are women. These women between the age groups of eighteen to forty-five are from the village itself and its nearby villages. This enterprise allows these women financial independence and empowerment.'

'Whether we believe it or not, even in today's India, the feminine gender remains grossly under-represented, undervalued and unrecognized. Our efforts in providing an employment source to these not so highly educated women of our country is a very small step to making them strong. They get trained by our experts, and over that receive mandatory vocational training of personal accounts to aid with their understanding of earnings, taxes and provident funds. We realized right in the beginning what we wanted was to revolutionize the lives of ordinary citizens, give them a better present and a hopeful future. These women we are empowering, as sales staff, as factory workers, as floor managers are going home and teaching their children values that aren't necessarily taught in schools. With one empowered, self-sufficient woman we are ensuring an entire family's future, an entire generation's well-being, resulting in a better tomorrow for India. These women will make strong mothers and strong mothers leave no orphans, make strong children and these strong children grow up to become a strong nation. Our initiative is towards the realization of the fact that as a society we need to grow up and start looking at women as an investment and an invaluable resource,' adds Ms Neha Khare, Director, Operations at GMD Enterprises Pvt Ltd.

GMD Enterprises runs a highly successful 100 MW solar plant at Bhiwadi, Rajasthan, and currently powers close to 14000 homes and 200 offices. It comes in at the 11th highest power supplier in India as of date.

GMD Enterprises is nominated at 'The Express India Inc Awards' to be held today at the Taj Palace Hotel in New Delhi.

The Durbar Hall was decorated in all its splendour today. Split in three sections, the stage at the front, bedecked with brilliant blue with LED panels on which the display kept changing as per the show flow. The seating area was split in two, three rows of round tables followed by theatre-style seating in the second section.

Rahul, Rehan, Jackal and Neha sat on one of the round tables, sharing their space with five other distinguished guests of the state—two union ministers, a media mogul, and a movie star and his wife. Their name plates shone in the muted lighting of the hall. The evening's hosts, a popular news reader and an entertainment television emcee, were inviting the CEO of India's fastest growing e-commerce retailer on to the stage to receive his award from the Minister of IT and Broadcasting.

The ceremony had been going on for 30 minutes now and had started with quite a glorious display of traditional performing artists from across the nation. Since the event was being recorded by a news media channel, there were large camera cranes roving overhead, panning across the guests and the presenters on stage.

What had caused quite a flurry towards the start of the program was the entry of the nation's Prime Minister, wearing a dark blue bandhgala, with his horde of advisors and security personnel. He had taken a seat at one of the round tables in the front and was accompanied by his Principal Secretary and the Minister of Corporate Affairs.

Neha and the boys couldn't believe they were only a couple of tables away from the most powerful person in the country. His eyes had lingered on their table for a second as he waved and folded his hands in namaste, before sitting down with his entourage, facing the stage. They were in the presence of the country's who's who—celebrities, media and corporate moguls, CEO's of the world's stage, ministers and TV personalities. The

India Inc Awards was a property owned by the *Indian Express* group, and was held every two years to applaud and award the best of the Indian Corporate world.

Being nominated for the 'Business Reformist of the Year' award had come as a massive surprise to the quad. They hadn't expected such a turn out in what was essentially their second year of operations, not counting the first three of the set up.

They were decked in their finest, Rahul and Rehan in fitted tuxedos, dark grey and black respectively. Rehan, looking elegantly stylish with his rimless glasses and short hair, cut specifically for the occasion. His ammi and Swapnil were sitting with Mr Bhatia and Mrs & Mr Khare at the back.

Mr Bhatia looked at his son, as the camera's panned to Rahul sitting at the table, looking incredibly dashing, even with his hair falling over his forehead. His suit and tie couldn't hide the gregarious and mischievous personality, but it could try, Mr Bhatia thought as he shook his head, smiling indulgently at his son.

Jackal made heads turn, as always, dressed in his finest all-velvet jacket tuxedo in deep maroon. His stocky, hunched figure, bald head and misshapen hand were accentuated in his choice of clothing, and he displayed them proudly, no more afraid of the stigma. He looked like a hairless wolf, on the prowl tonight. His excitement was palpable.

Mr and Mrs Khare were extremely proud of their girl today. She had proved her mettle in the world, like they always knew she would. Mrs Khare glanced at her daughter and thought to herself that biased or not, Neha looked ravishing in the black-and-white lamé and georgette sari she had on today; her hair swept to the side in her trademark look. She remembered with pride the second and third glances her daughter had received all evening, since the moment she walked into the hotel. *Beauty and brains, we are so blessed.*

Rehana Khan was dressed in a light grey salwar suit with a shining design at the border wrapped her head with a dupatta. She was having a hard time answering six-year-old Swapnil's inquisitive questions who sat starry-eyed and looked at every person on the hall with curiosity. Rehana Khan remembered Rehan's father who would have been extremely proud watching his son's success today. She wiped moistness from the corner of her eyes and with a smile looked at the stage ahead.

The emcees announced the last few awards of the evening a little while later and the excitement in the hall was palpable. The Hon'ble Prime Minister was invited on to the stage where he gave a speech about Corporate India and its resultant growth on the nation's economy and well-being. A hush fell over the audience as the PM waved his hand to stop the crowd from cheering and clapping.

As he folded his hands in a namaste, his deep resonating voice seeped into everyone present, 'Good evening to all present here. I am honoured to be here, and be a part of this prestigious event. I have always maintained, since taking office, that while our backbone may be our farmers and education, our strength has always been the corporate sector and I am so pleased today, to see such a wide calibre of start-ups, and organizations both old and gold, furthering the cause of India and all things Indian. For how long will we continue to become a nation of billion people selling cheap labour and raw materials, providing a large market for goods and services of other nations? Time has come that we become a nation where the youngsters are not the "job seekers" but "job creators". It will be my pleasure to help acknowledge and commemorate those of you who have exceeded all expectations and made India proud and marked us on the global map.' The crowd once again broke into applause.

As he paused, the lady from the wings walked up to him and handed him an envelope on a platter. The PM gently lifted it out and opened it. Holding the mike close to him, he announced, 'The award for Business Reformist of the Year 2015-16 goes to GMD Enterprises Pvt Ltd.' He placed the mike down on the platter. The cameras panned to show the exalted, proud faces of the four Directors of GMD Enterprises. The emcee was announcing their names and designations as the audience clapped for them. She then went on to describe the work they did Rehan, Jackal, Rahul and Neha stood up and walked the short distance to the stage in front of them. Rahul offered his arm to Neha as they both climbed the stairs after Rehan, led by Jackal. As they reached the centre of the stage to where the Prime Minister stood, all four of them bowed slightly in a namaste and reached forward to shake hands with the PM. He turned to pick up the trophy brought out by another hostess, while the four took a bow facing the audience, their hands folded in a namaste.

The Prime Minister indicated that they step forward to accept the award from him, as the flashes of a dozen cameras went off in front of them.

The host brought forward another mike for the team while his partner enquired if they would like to say a few words.

Rehan, Jackal and Neha looked at Rahul, and urged him to take the mike.

'Well, first on behalf of all four of us here, WOW! Thank you sir, Mr Prime Minister for this honour. This "Reformist" award is dedicated to the fifth and possibly most important member of our team, who is present with us, always in spirit, Major Ritesh Dhawan, who laid down his life for this nation in 2011. It is his life, his loss, his ideals and on his push that the four of us got together to follow our passion, think of giving back to our country and look for the well-being of others. Most of the times we fell short of our full potential in life as we don't have any role model. All four of us were living four different lives when Ritesh's demise shook us and made us rethink of what we were doing. We all got together behind our role model and started this venture. He was a man who followed his heart, believing in truth and power of one's convictions. To all those that knew him, you knew his one question to the world, *"Do you have it in you? GMD. Do you have it?"* It is in answering his question that the four of us found our calling. We would also like to thank and congratulate all the other nominees here, it is a great pleasure standing in your midst and receiving this award. Thank you!'

Rahul handed the mike back to the emcee while the audience gave them a standing ovation. The Prime Minister stepped forward again and put his hand on Rahul's shoulder.

'This, ladies and gentlemen, is the future of our country. Our hopes, dreams, ideas, and goals and strides towards development are riding on their strong shoulders. I am so proud to be able to lead a country that in the next decade that will be powered by 65 per cent of population below the age of thirty-five. I see a lot of youngsters that look to make their fortunes on distant shores, leaving behind their motherland in search of better opportunities. It is very easy to leave, very easy to think that your country's problems are someone else's issues. But it takes courage to stand up and be proud of your own house. Why would you want to go work to make someone else's home better? Why not put your hard work and efforts in creating a better environment, future for yourself in your own home? India is your home. We have to work together to make it perfect. Contribute to the development of your own motherland.

'I see the best of the best in this gathering here, proving to me and the world, that the talent of this country is beyond par and that our vision of a strong, prosperous and self-sufficient nation is in very capable hands. I want the achievement of these young Indians to be heard across nation and the spark of inspiration be lit from within. Thank you. Namaste.'

The GMD team on stage along with every other audience member clapped in response to the Prime Minister's words. He turned to look at the team kindly and proceeded to walk off the stage. His security joining him at the stairs, escorting him back to his seat.

Rahul, Neha, Rehan and Jackal walked off the stage receiving congratulatory messages and handshakes from those they crossed. As they got back to their seats, their companions on the table were giving them a standing ovation. They shook hands with them all and sat down to see the events wind up. The celebrity-actor next to Rehan leaned over and congratulated them all and proceeded to get his phone out and take a selfie with them, 'I'll be posting this on my social networks. You guys deserve to receive all the attention and support from your peers.'

After the ceremony was over, the team went out into the adjacent hall for the press meet. They spent 20 minutes intermingling with the media that wanted a sound bite from them on their win, they shook hands with the bigwigs of corporate India and made a lot of new contacts through networking. They could hardly believe the company they were in at that moment. Mr Bhatia walked in shaking hands with the people he knew and made a beeline towards his Rahul. He was more than proud today and couldn't wait to let his son know. The four of them hugged Mr Bhatia and posed with him for a photograph as one of the photojournalists ran up to them. Another journalist behind them came in and thrust a mike in front of them, 'Rahul Bhatia, you are the son of veteran industrialist Rajesh Bhatia, The Steel King, did you never think it would be easier to follow in his footsteps? Why did you venture out into your own when you could easily take over from him when the time would come?'

Rahul grinned and put an arm around his dad, 'The Steel King has very large footsteps, anyone following them would have very very large feet to fill. It was expected that I continue the family legacy and work with him, but my friend, having GMD is all about following your heart and your passion. Moreover if I would be Rajesh Bhatia, who would be Rahul Bhatia then?' he winked at the journalist.

'Ah, great. Thanks. But, ah... Could you tell me and I'm sure all of our viewers will want to know, what is GMD, if not the gaali?'

The quad laughed. Jackal stepped forward, 'Come my friend, I shall tell you all about GMD,' and led him away with his arm around the journalist. After ten minutes the reporter could be seen walking away from Dr Jackal his eyes shining and exuberating with purpose and clarity in life.

In the next instance, Mr Bhatia was surrounded by a few of his business acquaintances. Rahul, Neha and Rehan walked away. Rehan turned to the other two and said, 'Give me a moment, I'm going to search for ammi and Swapnil,' leaving Rahul and Neha standing alone.

Rehan hugged his ammi. Swapnil jumped on to him. Smiling Rehan hugged him too.

'Yeah Rehan bhaiya you won!' Swapnil said in excitement.

'Haha, yes Swapnil we won.' Rehan kissed him. Rehana caressed both of them, her eyes wet, 'Your abba would be very proud of you.'

Rehan smiled back, his eyes filled with tears of joy and accomplishment.

―⚏―

'Do you want to get out of here?' Rahul asked Neha, his face aglow with happiness. Neha looked into his eyes and nodded, 'Sure.'

Rahul held her hand and led her out of the hall. There were glass doors on the other end of the corridor and he aimed for the garden beyond it. He walked with a purpose, yet slow enough for Neha to walk comfortably without tripping on her sari. *Where will I start. There is so much to say...*

As he escorted her out into the garden, they walked a little way away from the hustle and bustle of the dinner set up on the other side of the wall.

Standing under the moonlit night, Rahul let the sounds of the crickets chirping fill up the silence. There was a beautiful scent of mogra flowers in the air intermingled with Neha's perfume, rich, deep and unique to her.

'Congratulations Rahul. Ritesh would be very proud.' Neha said softly.

Rahul opened his eyes and looked down into hers, 'How do you always know the right thing to say, Ms Khare?'

She laughed, 'What can I say? I'm gifted.'

Rahul laughed too and held her hand, 'Yes that you are. I on the other hand, an idiot.'

'I know that too.'

He laughed, 'All right, all right, smartass. Listen, I know this has been a long time coming, and I want to thank you for putting up with me since then, but I'm...'

'You don't have to say it.'

'No, let me.'

'Rahul, we both know you were an idiot back then,' she winked. 'But you have your moments.'

Rahul's pressure on her hand increased slightly, like he was trying to put his words into feelings. Neha tightened her hold on his hand too.

'I get it,' she whispered.

'Ritesh would have been kicking my ass right now,' Rahul said.

'Why?'

'Because I waited this long to do this...'

'Wh...' Neha started but Rahul placed a finger in front of her lips.

'Would you like to figure out the rest of your life together with me?'

Neha burst out laughing, 'Is this a proposal? For marriage?'

Rahul grinned, 'Are you mad? When I propose marriage, I'll be down on one knee with a beautiful ring in my hand for you. Although, I might have to go halfway around the world searching for a ring half as beautiful as you. No, this, this is a proposal for life. Someone very clever once said, follow your heart and it will never lead you wrong. This is me following my heart, and it's leading me to you...'

Neha looked at him and her lips moved wordlessly. She looked away and removed her hand from his. His heart sank. But in the next instance she threw herself onto him and hugged him tight.

'I accept your proposal, you moron!'

EPILOGUE

—⚏—

The office phone lines of GMD Enterprises did not stop ringing post the award night. The customer care center executives were flooded with phone calls and emails. Some of them were enquiring about the indigenous solar panel that the company has developed and some of them were enquiring about the team of women staff operating the solar plant.

Rahul, Neha, Rehan and Jackal were meeting in the conference room to decide on the next action plan. Their executive assistant walked in carrying a file in her hand. After making herself comfortable in a chair she said, 'The Gram Panchayat of a village Baansi in Chittorgarh District has offered us 25 acres of land to set up the solar plant in the village. The mukhia of the panchayat has sent a hand written letter to the board of directors of the company where he writes, "*Hamari gaon ki bahu betiya ab chulhe ke aage baith kar sirf khana nahi banayengi; wo ab desh banayengi.*"'

Everyone sitting in the room smiled. The small step that they have taken to change the society was now getting transformed into a giant leap by the entire nation. Dum, which was hiding in the fellow countrymen's gut, was slowly but surely showing its face.

She continued, 'We have got an invitation letter from the newly formed state of Telangana to come over and inspect the possible sites near the capital city of Amravati where we can setup our plant. We have got at least five similar proposals from all over the country.'

All four friends looked at each other and smiled. Rahul turned back towards the wall and looked at the framed photograph of Ritesh, Rahul, Neha, Rehan and Jackal. The picture was taken during their college days.

'Ritesh, its happening.' He resisted the lump in the throat while saying this. Neha placed her hands on Rahul's shoulder.

At the Same Time in the Reception

The receptionist has just answered one call when the phone rang again.

'Good morning, GMD Enterprises.'

Her face wore a stunned look when she heard the voice on the other side.

Yes...yes...okay okay...' she nodded her head letting the person on the other side of the telephone line complete. She kept the receiver of the phone on the table and ran towards the conference room in excitement.

She knocked at the conference room. 'Come in,' Rehan answered.

She walked inside the room and breathing heavily and said, 'Sir, there is a call for you from the office of the President of India.'

The four friends looked at each other. Excitement reflected on everyone's face. The time to start a new and long journey has come, and they were ready to hit the road ahead.

ACKNOWLEDGEMENTS

by Rahul Tiwari

I would like to extend my gratitude to the people who helped this book see the light of day; who provided support, talked things over, read, offered comments and suggestions, and assisted me in editing, proofreading, and finally getting the design of the book ready.

First of all, I would like to thank Tanmay Dubey who co-authored the book and helped me fulfil my dream of writing this book; this would not have been possible without him. Secondly, I would like to thank my editor Koel Mathur who did an excellent job, Vikas Pethiya who did the photography for the promo, Pankaj Shrivastav who helped me with the promo video, my brothers-in-law Ayush Khare and Karthik Raghuram, my cousins Anuj Awasthi, Harkiran Singh Chima, my sister-in-law Meenali Karthik for helping me with the promo video and Abhineet Mishra for his valuable inputs. Special thanks to my dear friends Shankar, Ashvarya and Kunal for their contribution in various ways, not to forget Advocate Rajul Shrivastav who took care of the copyright and legal matters. Above all, I would like to thank my family — my parents, my wife Meenal, my son Rishik who encouraged me to move forward. Last but not the least, I would like to thank Rupa Publications for doing a phenomenal job in publishing the final print for us and making my dream a reality.